THE HOSTAGE HEART

THE HOSTAGE HEART

Cynthia Harrod-Eagles

This first world hardcover edition published 2017
in Great Britain and in the USA by
SEVERN HOUSE PUBLISHERS LTD of
Eardley House, 4 Uxbridge Street, London W8 7SY.
First published 1997 in Great Britain under the title *Dangerous Love*.
Trade paperback edition first published in Great Britain and the USA 2018
by SEVERN HOUSE PUBLISHERS LTD.

British Library Cataloguing in Publication Data
A CIP catalogue record for this title is available from the British Library.

ISBN-13: 978-0-7278-8736-8 (cased)
ISBN-13: 978-1-84751-842-2 (trade paper)
ISBN-13: 978-1-78010-902-2 (ebook)

With love to Angie and Wendy,
who took such good care of my mother.

Author's Note

Dear Reader

When I was a little child, I was mad about ponies. Unfortunately, we lived on the top floor of a council flat in London, far away from riding stables and green fields, and my parents couldn't afford riding lessons anyway. So it was down to the local library for pony stories.

Ruby Ferguson, the Pullein-Thompsons, Monica Edwards – I gobbled them up. And when I had read every pony book in the library system, there was nothing for it but to write my own. Thus was born my impulse to write. Between the ages of ten and eighteen I wrote nine pony novels. Then at eighteen I left home and went to university, and when I discovered adult life held just as many disappointments, it was natural for me to start writing adult novels.

After winning the 1972 NEL Young Writers' Award with *The Waiting Game*, I began to develop ambition. I wanted to write a great literary novel; I wanted to win the Booker Prize; I wanted to feature in works of reference, for my books to be studied in universities.

But between a one-book Young Writer and great literary status there would obviously be a long and stony road. I was offered a contract to write three modern romances, and accepted it gratefully. A second publisher offered me a contract for another three, and a third for four more. I was developing the skills that can only come from *doing*, and making a name for myself in the publishing world as reliable and professional; and when that won me the contract for the Morland Dynasty Series, I was finally able to give up work and become a full-time writer.

This year will see the publication of my ninetieth book. I have come a long way from those first romances. I have not won the Booker Prize or written the great literary novel, but I have learned a lot, earned my living, and I hope, in my small way, given people pleasure. I still write two books a year. The compulsion to write is as strong as ever: life will always hold disappointments, and the escape into fiction is a comfort, for the writer as well as the reader.

This book is the work of a very young me; but it's the product of an energetic, enthusiastic and optimistic self in what seemed a simpler world, and I'm very pleased to see it back in print. If you know my later books, I hope you will uncouple your expectations, and just enjoy reading it as much as I enjoyed writing it.

Chapter One

The third time Emma saw the advertisement, she stopped and read it more closely. It had appeared in the *Guardian* and the *Times Educational Supplement* without causing her more than an amused glance, but finding it again in the trade journal she wondered if it could be serious after all.

It was the word 'governess' that intrigued her: so very Jane Austen, so unexpected in the nineteen-nineties.

Governess wanted to teach and care for girl aged 10. Large house. Other help kept. Excellent pay and conditions for dedicated person. Mrs Henderson, 3 Audley Place, W1.

It was the 'large house', she thought afterwards, that made her decide to write off. Not because she had ambitions that way, but because in conjunction with 'girl aged 10' it seemed to her infinitely pathetic. She pictured a poor little only child rattling round in a vast, echoing mansion. She had grown up one of seven – an unfashionably large family even in those days – in a three-bed terraced house in Hoxton. She shared a bedroom with her two younger sisters; her four younger brothers had the large bedroom; and Mum and Dad had the smallest room, which was only just big enough to take a double bed, so that their wardrobe had to stand out on the landing, a hazard to shins in the night when you had to go to the bathroom.

Downstairs was a front room – designated the quiet room

where homework was done – a back room where everything else happened, and the tiny kitchen. Outside in a minute square of garden the grass struggled unequally against an army of tramping, scuffing feet, for it provided the only play area apart from the street.

In this confined space they had tumbled over each other, played and quarrelled, helped and hindered each other; nine mouths jabbering, eighteen eyes precluding privacy, thirty-six limbs always in the way whenever you tried to move. Noisy it was, inconvenient always, exasperating often – but lonely, never. In moments of high irritation with the brothers who made a noise like a Panzer division when she was trying to revise for an exam, or the sisters who borrowed and spoiled her tights and her lipstick and her favourite sweater, she would cry out for peace and quiet and a room of her own. But she always knew how lucky she was to belong to so many souls. The old saying was: Home is the place where, when you go there, they have to let you in. When you had six siblings, you knew there would always be a lot of places you could call home.

So she thought how sad it must be to be a child, aged ten, in need of a governess. Was Mrs Henderson disabled in some way? Or was she away from home a lot? Perhaps she was in the Diplomatic Corps: Audley Place was Mayfair, where a lot of embassies were situated. A poor little rich girl, presumably. Well she would send off a letter and her CV, and see what happened. It would be interesting, at least.

Her flat-mates did not see it in quite the same way.

"Are you crazy, or what?" Suzanne said, staring at her over the coffee-tray she was bringing in. She was thin, dark and intense, with eyes that bulged slightly behind her rather John Lennon-ish, wire-rimmed glasses, and fine, straight hair that was always slipping out of its pins.

"What's crazy about it?" Emma said mildly.

"Going into service is crazy," Suzanne said, banging the tray down on the coffee table. "This is the twentieth century. Governess! You're not Jane Eyre, you know."

"Oy, look out!" Alison said, annoyed. She was painting her fingernails, her left hand laid out flat on a pile of books on the table which Suzanne had jogged. "You'll have the bottle over."

"Well, you shouldn't do that in here," Suzanne retorted. "It's disgusting. Some of us eat on that table."

"Blimey, I'm only painting them. It's not contaminating," Ali said. "It's not like Rachel cutting her toenails in the bathroom and leaving the bits all over the floor."

"One bit, once. Don't exaggerate," Rachel said, without looking up from the stack of homework she was marking. "I missed it. It wasn't deliberate."

"What is that colour anyway?" Suzanne said, staring now at Alison's hand. "It's nauseating. You aren't going to work like that tomorrow?"

"Of course I am," Ali said. "It's the latest thing: Amazon Green."

"Gan Green more like," Suzanne said. "Are you taking sugar or not today, Rache?"

"Yes. No, wait – make that no. I'll try without again." Rachel dieted on and off, though nothing she did seemed to make much difference one way or the other. She was a full-bodied sort of girl: not fat, but no Kate Moss either. Emma thought she worried too much, but Suzanne and Ali were both walking twigs, and Rachel looked at them wistfully when they swapped size eights and passed by the bra department without pausing. She took the mug from Suzanne and sipped it flinchingly. "Ugh! I wish I could get used to the taste."

"You don't persevere, that's your trouble," said Alison, waving her hand about to dry it. "Put two in for me, Suze. Anyway, go on, Em, what's all this about?"

3

Emma, who had been waiting patiently for all the sidetracking to end, passed the copy of the advert round for them to look at.

Suzanne frowned over it. "I'm sure I know that address."

"This Mrs Henderson a mate of yours, then?" Alison asked innocently. She liked baiting Suzanne.

Suzanne rose to it. "No, of course not. You don't think I mix socially with the types who live in Audley Place do you?" She had fiercely left-wing principles, and sometimes had difficulty in squaring them with her job with a top interior designer, where inevitably her customers were drawn from the ranks of the wealthy.

"Perhaps you did a job for her?" Rachel suggested soothingly.

"Maybe," Suzanne said, still frowning. "I'm sure I know the address, but Henderson — no," she shook her head. "It doesn't mean anything to me."

"So you've got nothing against the Hendersons personally?" Emma said.

"I don't need to have," Suzanne said. "You'd be mad to have anything to do with this. Even if it's genuine—"

"Why shouldn't it be?"

"Why should it be! Nobody has governesses nowadays. Nannies or childminders, maybe, for when they're little. Then the kid goes to school. Either there's something wrong with it, or the whole thing's weird. I wouldn't touch it with a bargepole."

"It's probably white slavers, Emma," Rachel remarked conversationally. "They'll drug your tea and whisk you off to the nightclubs of South America."

Suzanne raised her brows. "You think that sort of thing doesn't go on? I could show you an article—"

Alison intervened. Suzanne always had an article on every kind of human exploitation. "Well, anyway, you wouldn't want a live-in job, would you, Em? I mean, it'd make you like a servant. You'd probably get roped in for housework

4

and all that sort of thing. You know how people treat their au pairs."

"And running about after some horrible bratty rich kid," Suzanne put in, "who'll treat you like dirt—"

"Why should she be horrible?" Emma asked, amused.

"Bound to be," Suzanne said briefly.

"I agree with Suze," Alison said. "You'd be no better than a servant."

"Better a servant to one kid than thirty," Emma said. "Whatever this child's like, it can't be as bad as being a class teacher. I've had my fill of that, thank you very much."

Rachel looked up at that point. She and Emma had taught at the same school for three years, but Emma had given in her notice to leave at the end of this term. Neither of them had been physically assaulted yet, but they had endured most other things from the increasingly unruly children. "I know you want a change," Rachel said in her gentle way, "but isn't this a bit drastic? I mean, living in and everything, your time won't be your own. The kid'll be sick in the night and you'll have to change the sheets and all that sort of thing."

"Oh well, that'll be nothing new to me," Emma said lightly. "You forget I had six brothers and sisters. Anyway," she tired of the argument, "this is all a bit previous—I haven't got the job yet. I probably won't even get an interview."

And with that she changed the subject firmly, and a little while later when the conversation had picked up between the other three she slipped out of the room and sought the privacy of her own room.

Each of the girls had a bedroom to herself in the large, shabby flat in Muswell Hill, and they shared the living-room, kitchen and bathroom. The lease was in Rachel's name, but they shared the rent and the bills equally, and on the whole the arrangement worked very well. Of course, they had their quarrels. Suzanne tended to use other people's things without permission; Alison was very bad at clearing up after herself and had to be nagged to do her share of the housework; both of them tended to put upon Rachel, who was mild and gentle and would always sooner clean the bath herself than have an argument with the person whose turn it was; and all three thought Emma was neurotic because she couldn't bear dirt or mess in the kitchen.

But none of the arguments was serious, and the four girls rubbed along happily enough. Emma loved the flat. After her overcrowded childhood, it was paradise to have all this space, a room of her own where no one messed with her things; and after eight raised voices, three constituted peace and quiet to her. There was a big garden out at the back which strictly speaking belonged to the ground floor flat, but in which they were allowed to sunbathe and eat al fresco in the summer. And best of all, there were the wide green spaces and towering trees of the Alexandra Park right on her doorstep, so to speak. She was a Londoner by birth, a real townie, but she liked a bit of nature as much as the next man.

She could see the tops of the trees from her bedroom window, as she sat on her bed and started to prepare the next day's lessons. Her heart wasn't really in it, and she had to struggle to keep her mind from wandering to more enjoyable subjects. So she wasn't too upset at being disturbed when there was a tap on the door and Alison appeared.

"Are you busy? Can I come in?"

"Yes, if you like."

Alison leaned against the chest of drawers and fiddled with things. She was thin and red-haired and rather kooky-looking, given to wild clothes and outlandish makeup. Today she was wearing a leather miniskirt and a sort of sleeveless vest in purple lycra, and her hair stood out round her head in the through-a-hedge-backwards style which was currently fashionable amongst the bright young things. She worked for an very exclusive clothes shop in Bond Street which catered to the 'Daphne's' set, and blackish-green lipstick and nail varnish were nothing out of the ordinary there.

"Did you want something?" Emma asked at last.

"Oh, not really," Alison said, and wandered over to window. "Did you get the *Guardian* today?"

"Yes, did you want to borrow it?"

"No, I just wondered."

Emma waited patiently. Alison was never direct about anything. She was one of those people who, when you asked if they wanted a cup of tea, would answer, 'Well, are you having one?' Obviously there was something on her mind, but it would take a while to get to.

At last she said, "You know Phil?"

Phil was Ali's boyfriend. "That's a rhetorical question, I take it?"

"Well," Ali went on, "you know Phil works for British Airways? Well, he's got a friend who owns a travel agency."

"Really?" Emma said politely. Alison turned from the window.

"Em, you're not really going to apply for this job, are you?"

"Yes, I really am."

"I wish you wouldn't. I mean, I know you want a change and everything, but – well, why not make a real break, go into something else? I mean, teaching is bad enough, but this job you're talking about – I bet the pay's lousy, and the hours'd be terrible. What you want is a job that'll let you get out and about and meet people."

"And you've got something in mind?"

Alison looked eager. "This friend of Phil's – he's doing awfully well and he wants to take on an assistant."

"In the travel agency?"

"Yes. OK, he might not pay great bucks to start with, but it'd be an opportunity, because when he opens another branch, you'd be in line for manager. Plus you'd get all the cheap travel and holidays."

"And you think he'd take me on?" Emma said drily.

"I know he would, if Phil put in a word. They're great

7

's eyes pleaded. "Only, if you go for this
u'd be living in, wouldn't you, and you'd
d we'd have to get someone else."
na significantly.
, not the only reason," Alison said indig-
we all get along so well, it'd be terrible to break
.s up. I mean, we'd miss you. And I want you to be happy,
do the right thing. Will you think about it at least?"

"I'll think about it," Emma promised. "Thanks, Ali."

Alison idled her way out, and Emma stared out of the
window, thinking in surprise that she hadn't realised Alison
cared that much.

Only a few minutes later there was another knock on her
door, and this time it was Rachel who came in.

"Am I disturbing you?"

"No, it's all right." Rachel came in and stood looking at
her, chewing her lip anxiously. "Have you come to reason
with me too?"

"Oh dear, I suppose I have. Emma, have you really
thought about this? I know it's none of my business, but
it's an awfully big step to take. You'll lose your seniority,
and then there's the pension and everything. Teaching can
be tough, but you've got security, and jobs aren't easy to
come by these days."

"It's nice of you to worry about me," Emma said, "but
I've given in my notice now."

"Oh, but Mrs Petherbridge would let you withdraw that,"
Rachel said eagerly. "She was asking me today if I thought
you were determined to leave. She doesn't want you to go.
I don't either."

"Thanks. But I've thought it out carefully. It wasn't a
sudden decision, you know. I really do mean to leave."

"Oh. Well, if you're sure. It was just I didn't think you'd
be happy being a governess after teaching at a proper
school."

"I haven't got the job yet," Emma pointed out patiently.

8

"No," Rachel said, brightening. "That's right. You haven't. Well, goodnight, then."

"Goodnight," Emma said, and as the door closed behind Rachel she thought, whatever next?

Emma was the first up next morning, as usual. She was in the kitchen making tea when Suzanne appeared, which was not at all usual: Suzanne did not normally get up until half past eight, and was always last through the bathroom, since she didn't have to be at work until ten most days.

"Hello," Emma said. "Want some tea? It must be a shock to your system seeing the early morning light."

"Don't get smart with me," Suzanne said in mock exasperation. "Because of you I didn't get a wink of sleep last night."

"What, lying awake worrying about my welfare?"

"No, lying awake trying to remember why I knew that address in Mayfair. I just knew it rang a bell, but I couldn't put my finger on it."

"And you've got up at the crack of seven o'clock to tell me that?" Emma laughed.

"I knew if I didn't tell you I'd forget again and it would drive me crazy. It's Akroyd."

"What is?"

"Not Henderson, Akroyd. The people at 3 Audley Place. We did it up just before Christmas, but it was one of Simon's jobs, so I didn't have anything to do with it really, I just heard him talking about it."

"Akroyd, eh?" Emma said.

"You know about Akroyd, don't you?" Suzanne said suspiciously.

"Not a thing."

"Ignorant! Akroyd Engineering. You must have seen the name on motorway bridges."

"Oh, that Akroyd!"

"Yes, and *she*'s Lady Susan Stanley, the Earl of Cheshunt's

9

daughter. So they're rich as Croesus on both sides, I hope you realise." Her voice wavered between triumph and disapproval.

"Look, I haven't got the job yet," Emma said for the *n*th time. "So who's this Henderson person?"

"Search me. But anyway, at least you can let me know what you think of the house. It was a no-expenses-spared job and Simon raved about it. If you get to see inside, I'd be interested to hear your opinion."

"At last, someone willing to use the word 'if'," Emma laughed.

"I meant 'when' really. They're bound to want to see you," Suzanne corrected herself.

"Oh really? Why?"

"Because you'll be the only person bonkers enough to apply, that's why," Suzanne said, turning round and heading back to bed. "*Governess*! I ask you!" She turned at the door for a parting shot. "And if you get white-slaved, don't come running to me."

"I won't," Emma promised cheerfully.

Chapter Two

It seemed as if Suzanne's cynicism was justified, for Emma received a very prompt reply to her application, asking her to come to Audley Place. The letter was signed by Mrs Henderson and Emma liked the way it was phrased. It didn't sound at all like a job interview.

'I should be glad if you would come and have tea with me at five o'clock next Tuesday. If that should not be convenient, please telephone me, and we'll make another date.'

"Tea!" Suzanne snorted. "How fraightfully naice! What kind of way is that to recruit staff?"

"I don't know," Emma defended, "if you're going to have someone living in your house, it's important that you like them personally. Maybe you'd be more likely to find that out over tea than in an interview situation."

"She still doesn't say who she is," Suzanne went on. "I loathe that kind of inefficiency."

"Maybe she owns the place," Ali said. "Maybe *you* got the name wrong, have you thought of that?"

Suzanne gave her a dark look. "Not likely, is it?" she said, and stalked out.

"I wish you wouldn't tease her," Rachel complained gently. "You know how touchy she is."

"Oh, never mind that," Alison said blithely, "we've got more important things to worry about."

"Such as?"

"Such as what Emma's going to wear to her interview."

They both turned to look consideringly at Emma, who immediately felt nervous. "My suit, of course," she said. "What else?"

"Your navy suit?"

"Yes."

"With the red, white and navy scarf, I suppose?" Ali said witheringly.

"What's wrong with that?"

"It makes you look like British Airways ground staff, that's what."

"It was a very good suit," Emma protested feebly.

"When?" Alison asked cruelly.

"It's classic," Emma said. "It never goes out of style."

"True," said Alison. "What was never in can never go out. Why don't you let me lend you something?"

Now Emma laughed. "Have you looked in the mirror? I'd never get into anything of yours, Stick Insect."

Alison looked her over. "True. You are a bit of a Muscle Mary. Well, what can we do with her, Rache?"

"The suit's all right," Rachel said judiciously, "if she had it dry-cleaned. But she needs something better underneath it than a polyester blouse and that old scarf."

Alison's eyes gleamed. "Right, we can soon sort that out. Come up and meet me at work tomorrow and I'll find you something. And you must buy some decent shoes. Shoes are a dead giveaway, you know. If you've got decent leather on your feet, you can get away with murder, clothes-wise."

"Why, you dear old-fashioned thing," Emma smiled. "My grandmother used to say that back in nineteen fifty-five."

"*And* some decent tights," Alison went on firmly, ignoring her. "It's the first thing this Henderson dame will look at, if she's a real Upper."

"Just don't let Suzanne hear you talk like that," Emma warned.

In her room that night when she was getting ready for bed, she paused to study herself in the mirror. It was something she didn't often do. Usually she was rushing to get somewhere, and only glanced to see she was tidy, without really seeing what she looked like. She was accustomed to herself, comfortable with her looks; but now she stared and tried to see what a stranger would see. 'Muscle Mary', Alison had called her teasingly. Well, she did go to the gym twice a week, and she liked to keep fit, but she didn't think she was over-muscled, just nicely trim. And she had curves: she wasn't skinny like Ali and Suzanne, and sometimes beside them she felt practically gross, but in her heart of hearts she wouldn't want to be stick-like, however fashionable it was. She had nice legs, she thought. She would have liked her neck to be a bit longer; and she wished her hair was either dead straight or properly curly, rather than wavy and inclined to go fuzzy in damp weather. But it was a nice colour, what her mother called strawberry-blonde, which meant shades of wheat and barley and honey, naturally sun-streaked, and with threads of pure copper in it which gave it a reddish tinge in certain lights. Her nose was straight enough, her mouth wide, her eyes hazel. She was too used to it to know whether anyone else would find anything beautiful about it. She thought it was a pleasant face rather than a pretty one.

And besides, however much you might admire someone else's looks, you couldn't really imagine yourself looking like them; deep down, you couldn't really want to, because then you wouldn't be you. But she had to admit that clothes looked better on the stick-insects of this world, and there was nothing, she told herself with a sigh, to be done about that.

Audley Place was only a short walk from Marble Arch tube, and for a wonder it neither raining nor windy, so Emma had some hope of arriving looking tidy. She was glad Alison had persuaded her to improve her 'interview outfit'. The blouse she had on under the suit was pure silk crepe, beautifully cut and with a double-stitched collar and cuffs which enclosed

13

her neck and wrists softly and neatly. It gave you, she thought, a sense of confidence to be wearing something that felt as good as it looked. It was the same with the tights: she wouldn't have thought there could be so much difference in a pair of tights, but what she was wearing now was a world away from the usual old Marks and Sparks multipack jobs that she usually wore. Her legs thought all their birthdays had come at once.

The blouse had been horribly expensive, even with the discount Ali had managed to wangle for her, but just at the moment it felt worth it. Ali said that as long as she didn't spill anything on it she could probably take it back the next day: apparently it was called 'unshopping', and lots of people did it. Emma thought it didn't sound honest – and told herself that she could really do with having one decent blouse to wear with the suit on important occasions.

As she advanced into the residential streets of the most expensive real estate in the land, however, some of her confidence began to seep away. There was something *about* Mayfair! The houses looked so immaculate and so private; the little shops were so exclusive; and the further she got from Oxford Street the more select it became. The pavements looked cleaner, the cars more expensive – the very air seemed nicer to breathe. By the time she reached her destination she was feeling quite demoralised.

The red and white house was obviously freshly decorated, the enormous double front door under the pillared porch as glossy as dark water. Emma felt the house was staring at her with those tall dark windows, saying, 'What are you doing here? You're out of your league, girl – go back to Muswell Hill where you belong.'

Drawing her courage up from the toes of her shoes where it had slithered, she walked up the steps and rang the doorbell. She wasn't sure what she expected, but it certainly wasn't to have the door opened by a maid in a black dress and small white apron. A *maid*? She was really stepping out of her sphere.

While she stood trying to gather her scattered wits, the maid smiled pleasantly and helped her out. "Good afternoon – Miss Ruskin, is it? Please come in – Mrs Henderson's expecting you."

Inside the house was cool and dim, and smelled faintly and deliciously of beeswax. The floor was of polished wood, covered in the centre with a Turkish rug; the walls were panelled, and a staircase with a beautiful carved handrail curved upwards ahead of her.

"This way, please." The maid led the way directly upstairs. Underfoot the carpet felt like velvet, the handrail was so deeply polished it felt frictionless – it almost wasn't there at all. Emma was enjoying the sensations of the house so much she had forgotten her nerves, and when the maid opened a door on the first floor and announced, "Miss Ruskin, madam," Emma stepped over the threshold with an expression of confident eagerness which, though she didn't know it, gave her face a most engaging look.

She had only time to note that the room was well-lit from two large, tall windows, draped in voile, and observe the delicate pieces of antique furniture scattered about, before her attention was drawn to the woman seated in an armchair by the fireplace. She stood up with a ready smile, and at the same moment a clock on the mantelpiece chimed silverily.

"Ah, perfect timing! I do like punctuality."

"So do I," Emma said, smiling in response.

"Come and sit down, Miss Ruskin. I'm Mrs Henderson. Yes, you can bring up the tea now, thank you, Pam," she added to the maid, who nodded and went out.

Emma advanced across what felt like an acre of soft carpetings towards the slim, smiling woman, who extended a welcoming hand and took Emma's in a cool, firm grip. Mrs Henderson was probably, Emma thought, in her early forties, but was so exquisitely well-groomed she might have been either older or younger. She was dressed in a cocoa-brown jersey skirt and jacket over a silky blouse of gold-coloured fabric boldly patterned in black. Her dark hair was styled as only a hairdresser can do it and her make-up had been applied by a skilled and subtle hand. She wore no jewellery but an expensive-looking gold wristwatch and a plain gold wedding-band; and, applying the Alison test, Emma noted that her hosiery and shoes were impeccable.

Most of all, Emma noticed that Mrs Henderson *smelled* expensive. The air around her was sweet with the subtle tones of her make-up, her perfume, and the new smells of her clothes and shoes. No matter how scrupulous you were in your personal habits, you never got to smell like that on a teacher's wage and living in a shabby furnished flat in Muswell Hill.

"Do sit down," Mrs Henderson said, seating herself. "Tea will be here in a moment. Five o'clock's rather late for tea, I know, but I thought you probably wouldn't be able to get here earlier, if you were coming after school. What time do you finish?"

"Twenty-five past three," Emma said.

"And did you have far to come?"

"No, my school's only ten minutes from where I live."

"Well, I'm sure you must be ready for something after a long day coping with children. What ages do you teach?"

Emma had sent this information with her application, but she guessed that Mrs Henderson wanted to hear her talk, so she answered the questions easily, aware that she was being discreetly scrutinised by the woman opposite. But she was impressed that Mrs Henderson had arranged the interview so that she didn't have to take time off work, and had guessed she would be an aching hollow by the time she got here. Such thoughtfulness argued kindness, and Emma was comforted by that; and as the conversation advanced and she told her questioner more about herself, she felt that Mrs Henderson liked her, and was glad to have her here.

The maid came in with the tea-tray, followed by another bearing a cake-stand. Emma stared, bemused, at the kind of tea she had read about but which had never actually come in her way before: sandwiches cut into symmetrical fingers, hot scones wrapped in a napkin, and on the cake-stand squares of gingerbread, slices of Dundee and Battenburg, and a variety of small cakes.

"How do you like your tea, Miss Ruskin? Will you have a sandwich first, or a scone? A scone? Yes, it seems a shame to let them get cold, doesn't it? And which jam would you like? There's strawberry, raspberry and greengage. The cook makes them, down at Long Hempdon – that's our country place. Mrs Grainger is a cook in the old style, wonderful to say! How she finds time to make jam as well as everything else she does I don't know. We're always terrified she's going to be head-hunted and leave us, but somehow it never happens.'

Emma murmured an appreciative comment, and Mrs Henderson went on, taking over the burden of conversation so that Emma could eat and drink uninterrupted. "Well, I'm sure you'd like to know a little about the family. Mr Akroyd travels a good deal on business – he's Akroyd Engineering, you know – but the family lives permanently at Long Hempdon. That's in Suffolk, not far from Bury St Edmunds. Do you know Suffolk at all?"

"I'm afraid not."

"It's a lovely county. Will you have another scone? They're bought, I'm afraid. This house is really only a pied-a-terre, so we don't keep a full staff here."

"So it's Mr Akroyd who's advertising for a governess?" Emma prompted.

"Yes, for his youngest daughter. Ah, you're wondering how I fit into the picture. I wonder that myself sometimes," she laughed. "I was originally Lady Susan's social secretary – Lady Susan is Mr Akroyd's wife, did I mention that? When the family moved down to Suffolk Lady Susan didn't need

17

a full-time social secretary any more, but over the years I've added various other duties to my repertoire, including dealing with the staff. It's hard to define my position, really – a sort of house-steward, I suppose. I deal with all the things Lady Susan doesn't care to do herself. How is your cup?"

Mrs Henderson plied the teapot again, and then resumed. "The child who needs the governess is the youngest, Arabella. She's very much younger than her brothers and sister. The eldest, Gavin, is twenty-eight – he was the son of the first Mrs Akroyd. Then there's Zara, who's seventeen, the twins Harry and Jack, who are fourteen, and Arabella, who's just ten. They're all Lady Susan's children. So you see Arabella is rather isolated, especially as the boys are away at school."

"Wouldn't it be better for Arabella to go to school?" Emma asked, forgetting for the moment that if the child went to school there would be no job for Emma to apply for.

"Normally I would agree with you," Mrs Henderson said, examining Emma with her bright, curious eyes, which made Emma think of a Persian cat, "but Arabella is rather a special child."

Oh dear, Emma thought, here it comes. Everyone thinks their child is uniquely complex and difficult to understand. 'Highly strung' used to be the phrase – now it was 'sensitive'.

"She's very sensitive and highly strung," Mrs Henderson went on. "She was very unhappy at her last school, and fell far behind in her work, and what with one thing and another ended by making herself ill. What we need for her is someone able to 'cram' her so that she catches up, but that's not all. She needs someone to spend time with her, understand her, love her, and give her back the confidence she has lost."

"Yes, I see," Emma said, though she didn't, quite. What Mrs Henderson seemed to be saying was that Arabella needed a mother, and the question that naturally arose was, why wouldn't Lady Susan do? But she didn't quite know how to ask that. There had seemed some little reserve in Mrs Henderson's manner when she spoke about Lady Susan, which warned Emma not to probe.

After a moment, Mrs Henderson said, "I think I can tell you, Miss Ruskin, that I am looking very favourably on your application. Your qualifications and experience as a teacher are excellent, but more importantly I like you as a person. You come from a large family, and you obviously like children, and you come across to me as warm-hearted, affectionate, and level-headed. I think those are qualities Arabella needs. She's in danger of becoming a 'poor little rich girl' – of substituting material values for human ones. Your background – forgive me – is very different from hers. I think there's a great deal she could gain from you."

There was a silence while Mrs Henderson stared thought-fully at her clasped hands in her lap, and Emma finished off a piece of Battenburg and wondered what was wrong with the family and whether the 'sensitive' little girl would turn out to be a monster. Then Mrs Henderson spoke again.

"I've painted the picture for you as faithfully as I can. Now tell me, have I put you off?"

Emma said, "No, you haven't put me off. But I have to be honest with you: until I try, I don't know whether I can do any good for the child."

"But you'd like to try?"

"Yes," said Emma. "I'd like to try."

Now Mrs Henderson smiled. "Oh, I am glad! Because I want very much to offer you the job."

Later that evening back at the flat, Emma told the other three about the interview. About the child, she said only that she was ten years old: she didn't want a lecture at this stage about spoilt brats. Alison was impressed with the size of the salary that had been mentioned; Rachel by the friendliness of the reception; Suzanne wanted to know what she thought of the decorating job. But none of them was convinced that it was the right thing for her to do.

"Well," Emma said at last, "it has to be on a trial basis at first, until we see if I like the kid and she likes me. So if it's no good, I've lost nothing. I'm not committed."

"You'll have given up your job," Rachel said unhappily.

"I'd have given that up anyway. Seriously, Rachel, I don't want to go back to school, whatever happens."

"What about the flat?" Alison asked.

"I won't give up my room until after the trial period," Emma said. "I can afford my rent, don't worry. And while I'm away, if you want to use my room for overnight guests now and then, I don't mind. But this is still a bit previous. Mrs Henderson wants me, but I have to meet the rest of the family first."

"And when does that come off?" Suzanne asked.

"I'm going to spend Easter with them, and if we like each other all round, we'll finalise details them. If the worst comes to the worst, I'll have had a weekend in the country, all expenses paid."

"You sound happy," Rachel said. "You're really looking forward to this, aren't you?"

"Yes, I am," Emma said.

"Even the living-in bit?" Suzanne said curiously.

"Oddly enough, especially that. I like the idea of having the child all the time, not just for a few hours a day. If it works out, I can really make a difference."

"You're broody," Alison accused. "I know what it is — it's all a throw-back to Chris, isn't it? Getting so close to being married and then breaking it off. You want a substitute child."

"Shut up, Ali," Rachel said, unusually sharply for her. Emma was looking uncomfortable. It was eight months since she had broken up with Chris, but Rachel knew how much she had been hurt, though she never spoke about it.

But Emma said lightly, "It's all right, there's a grain of

truth in what Ali says, I expect. It'll be quite nice to be a surrogate mother for a bit: at least I can get out of it if I don't like it, which is more than you can do with the real sort."

The moment passed. Alison wanted to discuss whether Emma's wardrobe would stand the strain of a weekend in what she insisted on calling a 'stately home', and Suzanne wanted to tell Emma all the ways in which a rich child could be uniquely horrible, and soon they were all outdoing each other in bizarre fantasies about Emma's forthcoming stay in the country which wouldn't have been out of place in an episode of *The Addams Family*.

Later, alone in her room, Emma thought about what Alison had said. She had been very much in love with Chris, the first really serious love of her life. And she had thought he felt the same about her. At first everything had been wonderful: he had wanted to spend every minute with her; had planned a whole future with her; paid her extravagant compliments; told her he loved her a dozen times a day. He had never known anyone like her, he said; she was the embodiment of everything he had ever wanted in a woman.

But then he had changed, had started to blow hot and cold. One day he was wrapping himself in her arms, the next accusing her of stifling him. He began to hedge about getting married, asking what all the rush was. Emma, bewildered, could only stick to what she knew: that she loved him, and thought he loved her, and that if two people loved each other like that, they got married. That was so simple and natural, she couldn't understand what he found difficult about it. But on the day he first said he didn't think he was ready to make a commitment, she felt the iron enter her soul. These days, the word 'commitment' spelt doom to any relationship. It was the buzz-word of the emotionally irresponsible. Bit by bit, he detached himself from her, and in the process, painted her as a monster of possessiveness who had made life impossible for him. In the end, he believed his own propaganda.

Having broken off with him, Emma then had to draw back all the tendrils of love and trust she had put out to him, and learn to be without him – or, perhaps more accurately, to do without loving him. She had not been out with anyone since. When she was asked for a date, as she was from time to time, she made excuses. She did not want to go through all that again, and she didn't know, now, if she would ever be able to trust a man again. If she got fond of someone, and he said he loved her, how would she be able to believe him? Better, she thought, to stay single, and safe.

And in that case, going to live in a large house in the country might not be a bad idea, for she would be well out of the way of both harm and temptation. She had wanted a complete break, both from her work, and her social situation, and this job offered both. Some people might call it running away, but to her it looked like a sensible regrouping of her forces.

Chapter Three

Emma was the only person to get off the train, and there was only one person waiting on the platform, so there was no difficulty about their identifying each other. He was a little man like a jockey, in a dark blue suit; walnut-faced, with grey hair slicked back, which had a sort of dent in it all the way round his head, product of years of wearing a hat. So it was no surprise to Emma when he pushed himself off the wall against which he was leaning and said,

"Miss Ruskin, is it? Yeah, I'm the shofer, sent to meet you. Atkins is my name. Is that all your luggage? Right you are, then. Car's outside. This way." Emma was looking about for a ticket collector, but Atkins said, "Nah, don't bovver about that. Most o' these stations are unmanned 'cept in the rush-hour."

She followed him out through a wicket gate and into a narrow, green, damp, overhung lane. He chatted as he walked, as if he knew she needed reassuring. "Keep expecting 'em to close this station altogether, but we hang on by the skin of our teeth. Nearly lost it a few years back, but then our local MP got made a cabinet minister and the line got upgraded. Now we're starting to get commuters from Cambridge moving into the village, so I suppose we're safe. Good thing, too. 'Er ladyship wouldn't like it if they closed us down. She ain't been on a train in twenty years, but she'd have something to say all right. 'Ere's the jalopy."

It was an elderly beige Rolls, vast and stately as a ship, immaculate inside and out. Atkins opened the rear door and the car exhaled the smell of well-tended leather and freshly-cleaned carpets. Emma felt intimidated.

"Um, would you mind if I sat in front with you?" He looked at her, and she added defensively, "I sometimes get carsick in the back."

"Just as you like," he said, as if he knew she was lying, and opened the nearside front door for her and closed it noiselessly after her. He stowed her bag in the boot and then climbed in, picking up his peaked cap from the dashboard and putting it on with a just-audible sigh.

"Don't bother on my account," Emma said.

"Gotter wear me 'at. 'Er ladyship wouldn't like it," he said; but he seemed pleased by her remark, and set the car in motion with a faint smile lurking about his lips.

Emma felt she ought to use the journey to get to know him a bit better. After all, if she got the job, he would be part of her new life. "Is it far to Long Hempdon?" she asked to set the ball rolling.

"Five miles to the gates," Atkins said. "Then another mile to the 'ouse."

"Wow," Emma said, surprised. "It must be a big place. I wasn't expecting anything like that."

"Stately 'ome," Atkins said, and she couldn't tell if the comment was proud or derisive.

"Is it — was it — perhaps it was in the family, Lady Susan's family?" Emma hazarded.

"Nah!" he said robustly. "Guv'nor bought it fifteen year ago, give or take. Dead old, it is — Chooder mostly. *She* don't like it — draughty 'ole she calls it. Wanted a modern 'ouse. But *'e's* dead set on being lord of the manor. Wants 'is son to inherit the family seat and all that sort o' thing. He'll probably get a title from the Government next time round, see — services to industry, get me?" he added with a sidelong wink, "— so 'e reckons 'e might as well have the place to go with it."

"I see," Emma said. He seemed to be being pretty

indiscreet, considering she was a stranger, but it was all very revealing and she didn't want him to stop, so she asked, "What's it like, the house?"

"It's all big beams and little winders. All right if you like that sort o' thing," Atkins conceded. "I don't mind a bit of 'istory meself, as long as I've got central 'eating. Of course, we only use one wing. The family what owned it ran out o' money and it stood empty for years, going to rack and ruin. So the guv'nor got it cheap – he loves a bargain – and did one wing up. Going to do the rest up eventually, make it a show place. So he says. I wouldn't 'old me breath."

"And it's got big grounds, you say?"

"Any amount. Park land mostly – not much in the way of a garden. The eldest girl, she rides a lot, or she did before she went to college. Guv'nor always said she could ride all day and never leave her own grounds."

"The eldest girl – that's Zara, isn't it? What's she like?"

"'Oly terror. Like 'er ma."

"Oh," said Emma.

Atkins looked at her sideways, sizing her up. "New to you, all this, ain't it?"

"I've never had a live-in job before."

"It's different," he conceded. "Different way o' life."

She judged there was a gleam of sympathy there for her, so she said, "Tell me what everyone's like?"

Atkins faced forward again. "The Guv'nor's all right. I've known him donkey's years. I used to be a foreman at his first factory, down Chadwell 'Eath way. Then when he started to really make it big, he asked if I'd like to be his driver. I done that for about fifteen years, but it started to play on me 'elf, the long hours and everything, meetings till all hours then 'ome to pick up a bag and straight off to the airport. I got sick and 'ad to pack it in. But it was just about then that the Guv'nor moved down 'ere permanent, so he asked if I'd like to come 'ere as shofer, drive 'er ladyship about and whatnot. Well, it suits me all right. I got me own place and the work's nothing. So 'ere I am."

"It's nice to know that Mr Akroyd rewards loyalty," Emma said.

"Oh, he's all right," Atkins said again. "And 'is son's all right – Gavin – once you get used to 'is little ways. But—" He left the sentence tantalisingly open, and then deflected himself to nod towards the view from the front windscreen. "This is the village now, Hempdon Green. Not much to it, just the church and one pub. Used to 'ave a couple of shops, till they opened the big Tesco's over at Chevington Ash." They passed a village green, and came to a small humped bridge, beside which a road-sign said, 'River Ash'. It was a very small river, hardly more than a trickle, Emma thought.

"Runs into the Kennett," Atkins said. "Used to be fish in there – dace, chubb, pike as long as your arm. Now they got all them new fact'ries outside Bury, there ain't even any water in it. Took it all. No fish now."

"What a shame," Emma said.

They crossed the bridge. "All this is new," Atkins remarked. His mouth turned down. "Commuter-land."

He hardly needed to tell her that, as the last of the old cottages ran out to be replaced by raw-looking houses and bungalows with picture windows and open-plan lawns. And then they were out of the village altogether, and there were green verges and hedges to either side.

"Nearly there now," said Atkins.

Emma realised her chance to get information was running out. "What about the little girl?" she asked anxiously.

"Eh?" said Atkins vaguely.

"The little girl I'm supposed to teach. Arabella, isn't it? What's she like?"

"Poppy," he corrected. "Everybody calls her Poppy, except her ma. Yeah, she's all right. She can be a pain in the neck, like all kids, but there's no real harm in her."

He broke off. "Here's the park gates now," he said, turning the car in.

Emma looked eagerly about her as they drove up the tree-lined road. On either side there was grassland dotted with large trees. My own private Alexandra Park, she thought with an inward smile. At least I won't feel homesick. Then they rounded a curve in the road and the house came into sight. Emma gazed with some awe on the enormous, rambling Tudor mansion, not showing its disrepair at this distance. She felt dwarfed by the size of the house and park and the strangeness of the situation; and even Atkins seemed to have withdrawn into a grave silence, as if his alliance with her could not survive beyond the park gates. An enormous house; a 'her ladyship' who was a holy terror; a 'sort of housekeeper' – Mrs Henderson; a chauffeur and a cook, and so, presumably, other servants. She had never lived in this kind of way, and hadn't the least idea how to behave or what to expect.

Oh well, she thought, I'm only on trial anyway. I probably won't get the job, so what does it matter?

"'Ere you are, then," Atkins said, drawing up in front of some wide, shallow steps up to the front door. "You get out here – I've got to take the motor round the back. Don't worry about your bag – it'll get took up."

Another moment found her standing quite alone before the house and already visualising difficulties. Was she supposed to ring the doorbell or just walk in? How did she address people? Would she count as a servant or one of the family or what? She stood staring at the door and wishing she had never come; and while she was hesitating, the noise of a car's engine which she had been hearing in the background but which, being a Londoner, she had been ignoring, grew rapidly louder. Then a bright red Elan SE sports car shot out of the avenue with a noise like a growling dog, whirled into the open space before the house and screeched to a halt so dramatic that a handful of gravel was sprayed like machine-gun fire over the steps.

The engine was abruptly silenced, the door opened, and the driver extracted himself and strode, long-legged, to where Emma was standing. He eyed her up and down briefly and coldly and said, "I'm sorry but this house is not open to the public. You want Hempworth Manor, about a mile further down the road. That's the National Trust house."

Emma should have felt shrunken and humiliated by this display of cool arrogance, but oddly enough she didn't. She looked up at the extremely handsome young man with interest. She had never in her life seen anyone who looked so like a Gavin, and had no doubt that she was being addressed by the Young Master himself.

He was wearing a tweed sports jacket over a dark blue, open-necked shirt and beige cavalry twill trousers, all very expensive-looking, and showing off his fine figure to perfection. His hair was blonde, thick and springy like a Pantene advert. His skin had a golden tint that she felt was its natural colour, not the result of sun-bathing. His eyes were a vivid blue, the colour picked up and enhanced by the shade of his shirt; his features were exquisitely well-cut, firm and Grecian.

All in all it added up to just about the most handsome man Emma had ever seen, on or off the screen; and, boy, she thought, does he know it! His arrival in that car — and of course, it would be bright red! — with the screech of gravel, told just what sort of a bloke he would be: in love with himself, and expecting every woman to fall for him on sight. But Emma was quite unsmitten. He was so handsome he hardly seemed real, and she was simply enjoying looking at him. In fact, she probably stared at him for longer than was really polite. His nostrils grew a little white, and he said tautly, "I'm sorry, did you want something?"

28

Emma's sense of humour asserted itself. "Not really," she said. "I was just admiring your front."

He blinked. "I beg your pardon?"

"I've never seen anything quite like it." She paused just one beat and then nodded towards the house. "Your façade. Tudor, isn't it? Very handsome."

She could see he didn't know what to make of her. Tall, handsome, athletic and wealthy, he had probably spent his whole life receiving homage from other people, and being fawned over by young women; the idea that someone could be making fun of him, Emma thought, would throw him.

He seemed to take refuge in icy politeness. "You're Miss Ruskin, I suppose? Have you just arrived?"

"How clever of you to guess." Emma could not help herself, though she knew it was unwise to bait him further. She added hastily, "Atkins just this minute dropped me off. He's taken the car round the back."

"Then perhaps it would be a good idea for you to go inside," he said. "Allow me—" And he strode up the steps and held the front door open for her commandingly. She went meekly up and walked past him into the large, dark panelled hall; and saw, to her relief, that Mrs Henderson was coming down the main staircase towards her.

"Ah, Mrs Henderson, this young lady has just arrived," Gavin greeted her, with a hint of disapproval in his voice.

"I thought I heard the car," said Mrs Henderson with a welcoming smile to Emma. "Did you have a good journey?"

"Yes, thank you," Emma said.

Gavin cut across this impatiently. "Have Atkins put my car away, will you please," he said to Mrs Henderson. "I shan't want it again today."

"Certainly," Mrs Henderson said, and added quickly as he was about to turn away, "Have you been properly introduced, Miss Ruskin? This is Mr Gavin Akroyd. Gavin, Emma Ruskin, who we hope will be Poppy's governess."

29

Gavin inclined his body a fraction from the vertical in Emma's direction, but without meeting her eyes, and then took himself off without another word.

Mrs Henderson didn't seem at all put out by his coolness, and said to Emma, "Now Miss Ruskin, let me show you your room." She led the way up the stairs, chatting as she went about the train journey and the weather and so on. On the first floor she opened a door and said, "We've put you in here for this weekend, but of course if you do come here permanently other arrangements will be made. This is a guest room, you understand."

It was a charming room, beamed and low-ceilinged but quite large, with three leaded windows that looked out over the front of the house. The oak floorboards were wide and darkly-polished, the walls were painted pale primrose, which contrasted pleasantly with the dark wood, and the curtains and bedspread were a darker yellow, which made it all look very springlike.

"What a lovely room," Emma said with sincere pleasure.

"Yes, it is nice, isn't it? You have a fine view, too," Mrs Henderson said, walking over to the windows and pushing one open. It stuck a little, and she laughed. "You'll find out as you learn your way around that everything in the house is slightly skew-wiff – walls, floors and everything. It's impossible to hang a picture straight. But I always think it's part of the charm of an old house like this. And through here," she added, opening a door on the other side of the room, "is your bathroom – something the Tudors didn't have, and which I think is part of the charm of a modern house, don't you?"

Emma agreed. A bathroom to herself – what luxury!

"And now, my dear," said Mrs Henderson, "I expect you'd like to settle in and unpack and so on. Dinner will be at seven-thirty – you'll hear the gong at a quarter past. We'll gather in the drawing-room then for sherry – that's the first door on the right as you reach the bottom of the stairs. Now, is there anything you want before I leave you?"

There were a lot of things Emma wanted to know, but she didn't know how to ask them. It all sounded a little rich for her system – sherry, drawing-room, gong and all. Would it always be like this, or was this a special ceremony for her initiation? She couldn't think of a polite way to put that question, so she asked instead something more urgent.

"Should I change?"

Mrs Henderson eyed her skirt and blouse with understanding. "We don't dress," she said, "but perhaps you'd feel more comfortable in a frock."

Delicately put, Emma thought, and said, "Thanks," with a grateful smile, and Mrs Henderson left her.

At first she amused herself with examining her room. They seemed to have thought of everything for her comfort: a water carafe and glass, a box of tissues on the bedside table, magazines on a table by the window (*Country Life* and *The Lady*) – even a basket of cotton-wool balls on the dressing table. There were even plenty of hangers in the wardrobe; and an en-suite bathroom – just like a luxury hotel! She looked out of each window in turn and admired the view. Then she decided to have a bath, to use up the time until dinner.

In the bathroom she propped up her wristwatch where she could see it so that she shouldn't be late, and then relaxed in the hot water. There seemed to be no shortage of that, thank heaven! She had been afraid that staying in the country might be a bit short on comfort, but the plumbing all seemed to be up to scratch, which was a great relief.

Anyway, here she was, and in a short time she was to meet the rest of the family: her (possible) future charge – and why Poppy, by the way? – and her (possible) future employers. And Gavin. Hmmm. At any rate, it would be nice to have something around that was good to look at, though she hoped he would thaw out a bit, and not keep on

31

frosting her. She liked to be on friendly terms with everyone – but perhaps she shouldn't have begun by teasing him. It probably wasn't what he was used to, and especially not from someone he'd only just met. She reminded herself to be on her best behaviour at dinner – talking of which, it was time she got out of this lovely bath.

Drying herself, she caught sight of her reflection in the mirror, and made a face. "And now," she said aloud, "for the fray!"

Chapter Four

Emma walked across the hall and with a very slight hesitation entered the drawing room. She got the immediate impression of a large number of eyes turning on her; there seemed to have been no conversation going on, and she wondered for a hot and embarrassed moment if she were late and they had all been waiting for her.

But Mrs Henderson came immediately towards her with her hand outstretched, as if anxious to leave her no time to feel out of place. "Ah, Miss Ruskin! Do let me introduce you to everyone. Lady Susan Akroyd, Mr Akroyd, Mr Gavin Akroyd you've already met of course, and this is Arabella. And Miss Akroyd isn't down yet, I'm afraid."

"She's late," Mr Akroyd growled, and then approached Emma with his hand out. "How d'e do, Miss Ruskin. Can I interest you in a drink?" He took her hand in a hard grip and pumped it economically once up and once down, as if that was all he allowed. He was a short, stout man with the red face of a person who does himself well, but his expensive suiting and hair-dressing rendered the shortness and stoutness acceptable. There was perhaps a trace of Gavin's good looks in there somewhere, but they were spoiled by lines of bad temper or discontent. He was smiling at the moment, but it seemed a perfunctory smile, and his voice was harsh. He had a marked Lancashire accent which she somehow hadn't expected.

"Oh, yes, thank you," Emma began, but without waiting for anything further Mr Akroyd turned away saying,

"Sherry?" as he poured it out from a decanter on a small table. He put the glass into her hand with an air of having done all that was necessary, and retired to the other side of the room with his own glass, which was a heavy, short tumbler which obviously contained a large and undiluted whisky.

Emma wondered whether she ought to shake hands with Lady Susan, but being at a distance from that lady she needed some encouragement to cross what looked like a hundred yards of thick, soft carpeting. Encouragement was not forthcoming. Lady Susan, splendidly attired in a dress of blue silk and three rows of pearls, had not glanced at her. She was looking at her husband now with an expression of lofty tedium. Her style of clothes, hair and make-up made her look of an age with her husband, but stealing a sidelong look at her face, Emma thought she was probably quite a bit younger. Under the makeup she had classical features, but there was no animation in her face to make them beautiful.

Gavin was standing by the fireplace with a sherry glass in his hand, and his expression was only a little less unwelcoming than his step-mother's, though he had looked in her direction and bowed his head slightly when Mrs Henderson had performed the introductions. Now he stood broodingly, looking into the middle distance as if posing for a sculptor.

But there was someone else in the room who interested Emma more at the moment. The little girl had her eyes fixed on Emma's face with an expression of intensity, and so it was to her she went, holding out her hand and saying "How do you do," aiming for a manner that was friendly without being patronising.

The child took her hand after a moment's hesitation, seeming pleased with the grown-up attention. She was very small and thin for her age, and would have been pretty if it were not for the drawn look about her face, as if she had been ill for a long time. Her skin was transparently fair,

34

which showed up the dark shadows under her eyes; her hair was almost white-blonde, thin and fine and straight, and flat to her head. The hand Emma took in hers was damp, and the nails were bitten to the quick, but there was a little dab of pale pink nail-varnish on what bit of the nails remained.

Emma smiled down at her with a sudden piercing sympathy. "I'm very glad to meet you," she said, and meant it.

The little girl said abruptly, "I don't usually stay down for dinner. It's only because of you coming."

"Oh, well, then, I'm honoured," Emma said.

Unsmilingly, Arabella went on, "Zara said she didn't see why she had to eat now just because you were coming. That's why she's late. She wanted to have her dinner in her room and watch television."

Gavin said sharply, "Don't tell tales, Poppy."

Mr Akroyd coughed. "You'll find our Poppy a bit outspoken," he said, but it was not in apology. He looked at Emma defiantly to see what she'd say.

"Truthfulness is a good quality," Emma said, diplomatically.

"Hmm," he said, still staring at her. "Well, there's truth in what Poppy says. We don't often eat together when it's just family, but Mrs H thought it'd be the best way for us all to have a look at you."

"That wasn't quite how I put it," Mrs Henderson protested laughingly.

"Aye, well, that's what it came down to," Mr Akroyd said indifferently. "So if we're going to do it, let's get it over with. Gavin, ring the bell and let's go in."

"Surely we are to wait for Zara?" Lady Susan said. It was the first time she had spoken, and her voice was light and faint, but the disapproval was quite clear in it.

"Zara can damn well be on time, or go without," Mr Akroyd said. "I'm not waiting *my* grub for her." And he strode across the room and flung open the doors to the dining-room. Emma thought she saw where Gavin got his

35

assumption of superiority from. Mr Akroyd disappeared into the dining-room, but no one else had moved, and Emma felt very awkward, and didn't know if she was supposed to do anything or not. Mrs Henderson stepped in, smoothing things over, which Emma was beginning to gather was her main role in the household.

"Yes, well, it is half past, so I think we should go in, don't you? Gavin, won't you escort Miss Ruskin? Lady Susan, shall we go in? Come along, Poppy."

They passed through into the dining-room, which was dominated by a long mahogany table which would have seated twenty without a squash. It was laid now for seven, which meant that once seated they were so well spaced out that conversation was almost ruled out. Mr Akroyd was already seated at one end, and as Emma came in with Gavin walking stiffly at her side he called out, "Come on then, Miss – er – Whatsname, come and sit down here. Poppy, you plonk yourself down there opposite, then you can size each other up."

Gavin pulled out the indicated chair for her and Emma sat. She was on Mr Akroyd's left; the little girl took the chair opposite, on his right. Gavin then went to pull out the chair at the other end of the table for Lady Susan; Mrs Henderson sat on her left, and Gavin then took the chair next to Emma. Two maids came in to serve the soup, and the first deadly silence fell.

Even before everyone was served, Mr Akroyd had taken the first mouthful of soup. Then he paused with his spoon half way to the bowl and looked round the table; and, as if deciding that something was required of him, he said to Emma, "Well then, Miss – er – I suppose you want to tell us all about yourself. That's what all this fedaddle is about." Emma hardly knew how to reply, but he didn't wait for an answer. Instead he caught at the maid's arm as she passed him on her way out and said explosively, "Where is that girl? Julie, go up to Miss Zara's

36

room and tell her to come down right this minute, d'you understand?"

"Yes, sir," the maid said, and left the room hurriedly.

"Now then, where was I? Oh yes, tell us about yourself, Miss – er," Mr Akroyd went on, filling his mouth again.

"Herbert, must we talk business over dinner?" Lady Susan said severely from the other end of the table.

"Well, I don't know when else you think I'll get to see the girl," Mr Akroyd said, and put down his spoon with a gesture of exasperation. "In any case, I don't see why we have to have this fuss and nonsense. If Jean says she's all right, that's good enough for me."

"I'm glad to know you have such faith in my judgement," Mrs Henderson said, "but—"

"Right, then," Mr Akroyd interrupted. "Just ask this Miss Whatsname if she wants the job and be done with it."

"Ruskin!" said Gavin explosively, glaring at his father. "Her name is Miss Ruskin!"

Emma glanced sideways and saw his nostrils flare and a spot of colour appear in his cheeks. He was not leaping to her defence, Emma decided: he was angry and embarrassed by his father's rudeness.

"Whatever her damned name is, it's women's business to vet her, not mine. You just get on with asking what you want to ask and leave me out of it." And with that he attacked his soup again and had nothing more to say.

Lady Susan was ignoring the whole thing: she might have been alone in the universe, let alone at the dinner table. Arabella was moving her spoon about aimlessly in her soup, looking down at her plate with an air of withdrawn misery. Gavin and Mrs Henderson met each other's eyes across the table.

"Miss Ruskin has been teaching in a state school," Mrs Henderson said brightly and conversationally.

Gavin caught the ball from her. "That must have been

37

interesting," he said, turning to Emma. "What age group did you teach?"

"Middle school," Emma answered. "Tens to fourteens."

"I should think that must be very hard work," said Mrs Henderson.

"It is," Emma said.

"And demanding," Gavin added, looking at Mrs Henderson: *your turn.*

"But interesting," she said desperately. Lady Susan and Mr Akroyd continued to ignore everything.

Emma was wondering, half appalled, half amused, how they had ever got together in the first place, they seemed so ill-suited. She thought it was time she made a contribution, and said to the little girl, "I understand you are always called Poppy – why is that?"

She looked up briefly, and then down again. "Daddy called me it when I was little," she said in a small, embarrassed voice. "I don't like Arabella, so he said I didn't have to be it."

"Where the devil is that girl?" Mr Akroyd said suddenly, finishing his soup and slamming the spoon down in the empty bowl. It was impossible to tell if he had been listening or not. "Jean, ring the bell, will you? If she thinks she can just—"

At that moment the door opened and the missing member of the family walked in. She was slim and blonde, and would have been pretty except that her face was set in lines of sulky discontent. She had evidently taken a great deal of care over her appearance, which surprised Emma a little, given what Arabella had said about her not wanting to come down at all. She was wearing a very smart black evening skirt and pink lurex top, and her make-up was extremely elaborate for a family dinner. Was it possible, Emma thought, that she was trying to impress her? But why should she care what a potential governess thought?

"And where the hell have you been? You're late!" Mr Akroyd bellowed.

"I know," she said pertly, giving a defiant stare to Gavin, who was looking at her. She flounced in, sliding her eyes sidelong at her mother, who paid her no attention.

"Well, you'll get no soup now," Mr Akroyd said. "I'm not waiting for you."

"Good," she said. "I hate soup." And deliberately ignoring Emma, she walked round the table and sat down.

"Zara, this is Miss Ruskin," Mrs Henderson said, still trying to hold the evening together.

"Yes, I know," Zara said with elaborate indifference, shaking out her napkin. Emma, who had been prepared to say how do you do and be pleasant, subsided with amused despair. Was there no one with normal social manners in this household? Just then the maids returned to clear the soup plates and put on the second course, so there was an excuse for no one to speak for a while. Emma saw that Poppy had eaten nothing so far but a small piece of bread, and when she was served with a chicken breast in mushroom sauce she looked at it with something like despair. Had she been ill, Emma wondered? As soon as possible she must get Mrs Henderson alone and find out what was wrong with the child. But then she remembered she hadn't got the job yet.

With the chicken there were new potatoes, young carrots and asparagus: a simple, well-cooked meal. Emma was quite happy just to eat: she'd only had a sandwich for lunch and she was very hungry. Mrs Henderson seemed to have given up trying to make conversation for the moment, and Gavin was eating with savage concentration, his brows drawn down in a forbidding frown, while Zara was eating with elaborate unconcern. Emma looked at Poppy. She had made a pretence of cutting up her meat and was pushing it round the plate unhappily. She cut a small piece of potato and forked it to her lips, but then let it

39

fall off back onto the plate. At that moment she caught Emma's eyes on her; Emma smiled wryly – *that'll get you nowhere, you know* – and the child suddenly blushed guiltily.

"Now Miss Ruskin's here, can I go riding again?" she asked, as if to distract attention. She added quickly to Emma, "I haven't been for ages because there was no one to take me and I'm not supposed to go out on my own."

Emma could not ignore such a plea for help. "Do you have your own pony?" she asked.

The pinched face lightened a little. "Yes, he's called Misty and he's white—"

"You mean he's a grey," Zara said witheringly. "You don't talk about *white* horses – you ought to know that at your age."

Poppy's face reddened. "I don't care. I shall call him white because he *is* white," she said defiantly.

"Well, you'll just show your ignorance, then," Zara said. "Anyway, I don't suppose for a minute she can ride," she added, with a flick of a glance in Emma's direction. "Why should she, where she comes from?"

Poppy turned an eager gaze on Emma. "You can, can't you? I bet you can."

"I did learn to ride when I was a child, but I haven't done it for ages. Still, I don't suppose it's something you forget, is it?"

"Where did you learn?" Mrs Henderson asked, hoping to keep the conversation polite.

"In Epping Forest. I had a course of lessons at a riding school when I was about twelve."

"I knew you could," Poppy said gratefully. "So I can go riding again, can't I? She can come with me?" She looked from mother to father, neither of whom was listening, and then appealed to Mrs Henderson. "Can't I?"

Zara jumped in sharply. "And what do you think she's

40

going to ride? I hope you don't think she's going to ride *my* horse?"

"Well, why not?" Poppy said defiantly.

"Don't be ridiculous. She couldn't manage him. Besides, I might want him."

"But you haven't taken him out for weeks."

"She couldn't possibly ride well enough. I'm not having Barbary's mouth ruined by a beginner."

Emma raised her eyebrows at this unprovoked rudeness, but she said peaceably, "Perhaps I could come with you on a bicycle?"

Zara addressed her directly for the first time. "We haven't got any bikes," she said with childish triumph.

"I'll *buy* a bloody bike!" Mr Akroyd bellowed suddenly, making everyone jump, and Lady Susan drew an audible breath of disapproval. He glared up and down the table. "Now let's have an end to this bloody yattering and arguing! You're like a pack of hyenas, the lot of you! Julie, clear these plates away."

The table was cleared and Emma found herself being offered a choice between raspberry sorbet and chocolate pudding. She was about to ask for sorbet when Zara said loudly, "Good heavens, the sorbet, of course. The pudding's kid's stuff. It's only meant for Poppy."

Some devil in Emma made her say to the maid who was hovering by her, "Chocolate pudding for me, please. I love all pudding, but chocolate's my favourite." The maid served her with, Emma could have sworn, a smile hovering about her lips.

"Good lord, how vulgar," Zara said, staring down the table at Emma's plate.

And immediately Gavin said, "I'll have the pudding as well, please."

"But you never eat pudding!" Zara cried, as though cheated.

"I can change, can't I?" Gavin said.

41

"You haven't changed. You don't like pudding," Zara insisted suicidally.

"Then I must have some other reason. I leave it to you to decide what it might be," Gavin said.

He levelled a very frosty look at his half-sister. Her cheeks reddened, and she opened her mouth to retort, but Mr Akroyd looked up from his plate and said, "If anyone else says the word 'pudding', they go out of this room. It's like a bloody madhouse in here tonight."

In the silence which followed Emma realised that Lady Susan at the other end of the table had not yet announced her choice, and for a breathless, almost hysterical moment she imagined what would happen if her ladyship opted for the chocolate pud. But of course she did nothing so vulgar. She merely waved the maid away and snipped herself some grapes off the elaborate stand of fruit which decorated the table.

The meal soon came to its close; they all filed through to the drawing-room for coffee, and Emma wondered how soon she could escape to her room. The Family From Hell, she thought to herself: the scenes over dinner had been so grisly it was almost funny. Mr Akroyd evidently felt he had done enough of the polite, for he bolted his coffee and with a muttered excuse hurried out of the room. Zara went over to the hi-fi in the corner and began fiddling about with CDs, looking for something to put on – presumably something that would annoy as many people as possible, Emma thought.

Lady Susan, having received her coffee, suddenly looked towards, though not at, Emma, and said, "Do you hunt, Miss Ruskin?"

Emma couldn't help herself. "Hunt what?"

Zara turned and threw a contemptuous look in Emma's direction. "Oh my God," she muttered sneeringly.

But Emma had no desire to join the tribal rite of rudeness, so she corrected her reply hastily to, "No, I'm afraid not. I've never had the chance."

Lady Susan digested this without emotion. She tried again. "Are you by any chance related to the Norfolk Ruskins?"

"I'm afraid I don't know," Emma said. "My father came from Hoxton. That's where I was born."

"Hoxton?" Lady Susan enquired with a vague frown. "And where—?"

"It's in the east end of London," Emma told her. Lady Susan's eyes widened slightly as if she had said something indecent, and then she turned her head away and began talking to Mrs Henderson in a low voice. Snubbed again, Emma thought. She was growing almost merry on discomfiture, as though it was intoxicating.

And then suddenly Gavin was by her side, sitting, coffee cup in hand, on the sofa beside her and saying politely, "I wonder, Miss Ruskin, if you would care to come to church with us tomorrow morning? The car will hold one more. We go to the parish church in the village, and it's always rather a nice service on Easter Day."

"Yes, thank you, I'd love to," Emma said, glad of a kind word at last.

"Are you a churchgoer?"

"Well, I'm C of E as far as I'm anything, but I haven't been for years," Emma said. "I don't think people do, much, in London."

"What has London got to do with it?"

"Oh, I don't know – it's just a different sort of life from the country, isn't it? I mean, in a village, the church is part of the way of life. You don't have that sort of community in London."

"And do you think that's a sufficient reason for going to church?" he asked. She couldn't tell if he were disapproving or not.

"Everyone has to work that out for themselves," she said. "I shall enjoy the singing and the atmosphere – that will be reason enough for me to go."

43

"You're very straightforward, aren't you?" he said, but again, neutrally.

"I try to be. It saves a lot of time and confusion," she said. "But isn't bluntness an Akroyd trait? So your father was saying, anyway."

He didn't answer that, only looked at her with a faint, speculative frown. Blotted my copybook again, she thought. Oh, the hell with it!

They were interrupted by Mrs Henderson. "I think it's time Poppy was in bed now," she said, standing up. "You look rather tired too, Miss Ruskin," she added, giving Emma the chance to escape. Emma took it gratefully, and said goodnight all round. Zara and Lady Susan did not respond, but Gavin stood up politely and said, "Breakfast for churchgoers is at eight. Please let Mrs Henderson know what time you'd like to be called and she'll arrange it."

"Thank you," Emma said, and followed Mrs Henderson and Poppy out of the room. At the first floor their ways parted. Emma looked down at the little girl's peaky face and said, "Goodnight, then, Poppy – may I call you Poppy?"

Poppy nodded. "Will you still be here tomorrow?" she asked.

"Yes, of course. Didn't you hear me say I'll be coming to church?"

"Yes, but people say things," she said cryptically, "and then they don't do them."

"I will certainly be here tomorrow. I'll see you at breakfast."

Poppy regarded her face seriously for a moment, and then nodded again, with satisfaction, though unsmiling. "G'night then."

Alone in her room, Emma could not immediately settle. She paced up and down, going over the evening in her head and trying to sort out the impressions of this most unfamilial family. What a bunch of charmers! she thought. You'd have to be mad to want to be part of this set-up.

44

Then she thought of the pale and miserable child making circles with her spoon in her soup. No one seemed to care for her, she thought; and she felt a fierce longing to make things right for her. But she had probably blown her chances of the job. She'd be on her way on Monday evening with a flea in her ear – if they didn't throw her out tomorrow.

There was a tap on the door of her room, and she went to open it, and found Mrs Henderson standing without, looking embarrassed. "Oh Miss Ruskin, I'm glad you're still up," she said in a rush, as though she wanted to get it over with. This is it, thought Emma. She's going to ask me to pack my bags. "I – I do hope you didn't get too bad an impression of us," Mrs Henderson said. She laughed nervously. "I'm afraid it wasn't the most convivial of evenings."

"Oh, no, really," Emma began, trying to find a polite response. "I – er – the dinner was very nice."

Mrs Henderson hurried on. "The thing is, Poppy really took to you. She was talking about you while we were walking upstairs, and she was quite excited at the idea of having you for her governess. And the poor child really does need someone of her own. I do hope – I mean, I suppose – have you come to any conclusions about the job?"

"I didn't think I needed to," Emma said. "I was sure I wouldn't be offered it. I didn't make much of an impression on Lady Susan."

"Oh, I shouldn't worry about that, if I were you," Mrs Henderson said. "Lady Susan won't really trouble herself about it, and you heard Mr Akroyd say that he would abide by my decision. It's Gavin who will really have the final say."

Emma was so surprised by that she didn't manage to ask why. Mrs Henderson hurried on. "If you were to be offered the job, would you still consider it?"

45

"Oh yes," Emma said, "I'd certainly consider it." She surprised herself a little with how firmly it came out.

"I'm glad," said Mrs Henderson, and said goodnight and turned away and left her.

Chapter Five

After the emotional turmoil of the evening before, Emma slept badly, and woke with the frightening sense of someone being in the room. A moment later the curtains were drawn back with a sound which, in her state of half-wakefulness, was like the ripping of metal foil. It made her sit up with a gasp of shock.

"Oh, sorry miss, did I frighten you?" It was a young woman, a stranger. Emma stared at her blankly, hardly knowing where she was. "It's half past seven. I've brought you some tea."

"Oh! Yes, thank you." Reality slowly tuned in. She was at Long Hempdon, and she was being woken up by a maid. Imagine! With memories of old books she had a sudden horrible doubt whether the maid would want to lay out her clothes, but she only smiled and went out, closing the door soundlessly behind her. Emma reached for the tea and sipped gratefully. Outside the sun was shining, and several thousand birds seemed to be cheeping and whistling and chirruping in satisfaction over the fact. It was a far cry from Muswell Hill, where the birds had to compete with the traffic noise.

"Why did I ever live in town?" she asked herself as she jumped out of bed and headed (oh sinful luxury!) for her own private bathroom, which would not have any of Ali's tights dripping from the shower-rail, or Suzanne's talcum powder coating every surface.

When she reached the breakfast table she found Mrs Henderson, Gavin and Poppy already seated and eating.

Gavin was reading the business section of the *Sunday Times*, and Mrs Henderson was listening to Poppy who was describing the Easter eggs she had found at her bedside when she woke.

"I've eaten two Rolo mini-eggs already, and a whole Buttons egg *and* the buttons, and half a Cadbury's creme egg," Poppy was saying as Emma came in. "It's nearly as good at Easter as it is at Christmas!"

"You'll be sick, you little horror," said Gavin without looking up from the paper.

"I'm never sick with chocolate, only with dinner and spinach and liver and things like that," Poppy said.

"Good morning, Miss Ruskin. Did you sleep well?" Mrs Henderson noticed her at that point. With a friendly nod she indicated the empty place beside Gavin.

"Yes, thank you," Emma said, taking the seat, and wondered why people always asked that and why you always lied when you hadn't slept well. Gavin only flicked a glance at her and returned to the paper, as though determined not to notice her; Poppy gave her a shy smile and concentrated on pushing her spoon into her boiled egg without letting the yolk spill over.

"Can I pour you some coffee?" Mrs Henderson offered.

"Yes, thank you." Emma felt it was up to her to make some polite conversation. "Isn't it a lovely day? I was thinking when I woke up how nice it is to be in the country on a day like this."

She thought that must be unexceptionable, and Mrs Henderson smiled and seemed about to make some polite reply, but Gavin folded his paper to a new page with a great deal of rattling and said coolly, "I'm afraid your reading of the weather signs is not quite accurate, Miss Ruskin. We will certainly be having rain in an hour or two."

"Oh, surely not," Emma protested brightly, deciding he was just being perverse. "With that blue sky and those pretty white clouds—"

48

"A sky that colour is not to be trusted at this time of year," he said without even looking at her, "and those pretty clouds are from the west, which always means rain."

"Perhaps Miss Ruskin doesn't have much opportunity to study the weather, living in London," Mrs Henderson said soothingly.

Gavin looked at her with a raised eyebrow. "Are you trying to suggest that they don't *have* weather in London?"

Mrs Henderson frowned at him, and Emma said cheerfully, "I don't even know which way west is." If they wanted her to be an ignorant townie, then she would act up to them.

Poppy looked shocked. "Oh, but you must know that! East is where the sun rises and west is where it goes down. Everybody knows that. I've known that since I was *born*, nearly!"

"I only know east from west on a tube map," Emma said.

"What's a tube map?" Poppy asked blankly.

"There you are, you see, even you don't know everything," Mrs Henderson said to Poppy reprovingly. "You may be at home in the country but you'd be lost in London. Do you like a cooked breakfast, Miss Ruskin?" she hurried on, as if determined to change the subject. "I'll ring if you would like bacon and eggs or anything of the sort."

Emma was going to say no, rather than be any trouble, but sensing that Gavin was looking at her, waiting for her answer, she decided, what the hell, she'd be as much trouble as possible and enjoy herself. If he was going to disapprove of her anyway, she might as well get something out of the weekend.

"Yes, please. I like to breakfast in style on a Sunday. I don't generally have time on school days for more than a piece of toast."

The breakfast was excellent, and Emma wolfed everything, while Gavin worked his way through the paper, Mrs

Henderson described the architecture of the local church, and Poppy wriggled with boredom. Emma was happily crunching toast and marmalade when the door opened and Zara came in.

"Morning. Not too late, am I?" she said, dropping into the seat beside Poppy, who was staring at her with unconcealed amazement.

"Too late? No, of course not," Mrs Henderson said, seeming a little surprised herself. "Shall I ring? Would you like something hot?"

"Good God, no!" Zara exclaimed with a theatrical shudder. "What kind of person d'you think eats all that bacon and eggs muck these days? Just shove me over a piece of toast, will you?"

"I'd happily shove you over the nearest cliff," Gavin said, glaring at her over the News Review section. "What are you doing down at this time of the morning, anyway?"

Zara looked defiantly at him. "I'm coming to church with you, of course. It *is* Easter."

"Oh Zara, you never go to church," Poppy said reproachfully. "When Gavin got cross with you last time, at Christmas, you said it was boring and stupid, and he said well then there was no point in you going if you felt like that, and you said—"

"Shut up, nobody asked you," Zara said quickly.

"Maybe they didn't, but she has a point," Gavin said. "Why the sudden change of mind?"

Under his steady scrutiny Zara coloured a little. "What does it matter why I've changed my mind? I have, that's all. Anyway, you're always so holy about it, you ought to be glad I want to come."

"Yes, well, normally I would rejoice over the return of a sinner to the fold," Gavin said drily, "but you know perfectly well Dad's gone out in the Mercedes and Atkins has taken the Rolls over to Cold Ashford. We're going in Mrs H's Mini, and that only takes four."

"Well, that's all right," Zara said, concentrating on buttering her toast, "Miss Whatsername can stay at home. I don't suppose she really wants to go. She said last night that she never does normally."

Poppy opened her mouth to point out the illogic, but Gavin spoke first. "The fact remains that there are only three spaces in the car," he said calmly, "and Miss Ruskin laid her claim first."

"Laid her claim? What on earth are you talking about?" Zara said scornfully. "Last night she said she wanted to go because there was a spare place in the car. Now there isn't a spare place in the car, she can stay at home. What's all the fuss about?"

There was a brief silence while Emma wondered what she had done to earn this resentment from a girl she barely knew, and struggled against the urge to say she would stay home, just to avoid more argument. Gavin began to fold up his newspaper with an air of finality.

"There's no fuss at all. If you really want to go, you can go in the Mini with Mrs H and Poppy, and I'll take Miss Ruskin in my car."

He pushed back his chair and walked briskly from the room before anything more could be said. As he passed Emma's chair she saw the tightly compressed lips and frown of annoyance, and thought, with a sinking heart, what a jolly drive they would have of it. Though it was Zara's doing, he was bound to blame her for the disturbance of his peaceful breakfast and the nuisance of having to take two cars. She had not made a good impression on this family so far – but, really, who could have?

Zara had the grace to look a little subdued at her brother's exit, but Poppy was wide-eyed and garrulous. "Oh, it's not fair! Oh, you lucky thing! I've been asking Gavin for ages to drive me in his car but he won't take me. He drives ever so fast, and Mummy says he'll kill himself one of these days, but I bet he won't."

51

"Shut up, Poppy," Zara growled.

"Well, he won't," she said defiantly. "Daddy says no son of *his* is a bad driver, and he's had the Elan a year and never got a scratch on it, so he must be good, because the Mini's got dents all over, and Daddy says that's because of Mrs H touch-parking. What's touch-parking?"

"Poppy, stop gabbling and drink your milk," Mrs Henderson said, catching Emma's eye and suppressing a laugh.

Poppy stuck out her lip. "I don't like milk. Why can't I have tea?"

"Because milk's better for you," Mrs Henderson said with the weary air of one who has covered this ground before. Emma noticed that very little of the boiled egg had gone down Poppy's throat, and wondered whether it was because of all the chocolate eggs, or from the same cause as last night's uneaten dinner. But Poppy was gathering herself for an argument, and Emma thought she ought not to be there to witness it, in case it turned Poppy against her as well.

"I think I'll go and tidy up, if you'll excuse me," she said, and fled the fractured family with as much dignity as she could muster.

Her forecast of the journey to church was right: Gavin drove in grim silence, his eyes never straying from the road ahead, as if he was determined to get this tiresome task over with. Emma's sense of mischief roused itself. She *would* make him talk! She began to ask him questions about anything that came into her mind: what are those birds over there? Oh, I see, and what's the difference between a rook and a crow? And is a west wind one that blows from the west or to the west? And what sort of trees are those?

Gavin answered her as abruptly as possible, until she over-reached herself and asked what were those flowers, pointing at random and happening to alight on a verge full of blowing yellow trumpets.

"Daffodils," he said shortly, glancing at her sidelong.

"I suppose you want to tell me you don't have those in London."

"Oh, but you see," Emma said brightly, "country daffodils are so much bigger than town daffodils."

A flush spread across Gavin's beautiful cheekbones, and his eyes were fixed on the road again. "I don't know what sort of game you think you're playing, but I suppose you think it's clever to amuse yourself at others' expense. We may live in the country, but we're not exactly stupid, you know."

"I didn't think you were," Emma said, half contrite, half annoyed. "It was just a joke."

"Oh, a joke, was it?" Gavin swung the car backwards into a space alongside the churchyard wall. "Pardon me, but I thought the point of a joke was that it was supposed to be funny."

Emma's contrition died the death. What a pompous prig, she thought. He got out of the car without another word and came round to her side to let her out. No one is at their best struggling up from the low seat of a sports car, but she would not take advantage of his offered hand. She extricated herself with as much dignity as she could muster, waited while he put the hood up on his car, and then walked ahead of him into the church. They sat side by side on a pew near the front, waiting for the others to arrive, while the organist played a voluntary; and she resolved she would not bother to talk to him again unless she had to. The whole weekend was a disaster, and if it really was Gavin who had the final say, she obviously wasn't going to get the job.

But the church was very beautiful, and it was Easter Sunday after all, and she felt she ought not to be sitting here in this resentful frame, so she cleared her mind of all negative thoughts and concentrated on enjoying the sights and sounds around her. Out of the corner of her eye she saw Gavin glancing at her out of the corner of his, and

53

wondered whether he was sorry he had made so much fuss. Well, she wouldn't give him the satisfaction! But no, that was negative again. She composed her expression and looked at him, ready to be friendly, but he was looking straight forward again and would not meet her eye, so she shrugged inwardly and dropped it.

When they came out of the church after the service, Emma found to her surprise and annoyance that Gavin had been right about the weather. His prophecy had been fulfilled. The whole sky had clouded over, and the rain was just beginning, driven in large scattered drops by a brisk wind – a west wind, presumably, she thought sourly.

"Oh blast," Poppy said. "I wanted to show you the stables and my favourite ride this afternoon."

"It's going to tip down any minute. It's a good job I put the hood up," Gavin said pointedly; but Emma thought he was entitled to an *I told you so* and that this was a pretty restrained one in the circumstances.

"We're holding up the traffic standing here," Mrs Henderson said, coming up behind them in the porch. "I think we ought to get moving. Where's Zara?" She was lingering behind talking to a friend. "Poppy, go and ask her to come along, would you?"

Zara came up to them with two other girls of her own age, both pretty and smartly dressed, and with eyes that seemed drawn to Gavin like pins to a magnet, no matter who they were addressing. Well, it was natural, Emma thought. He was extremely easy on the eye.

"Natalie and Victoria are coming back with us for lunch," Zara announced brightly as she reached the group.

"It's awfully nice of you to invite us," Natalie said. "It's awful at home on Sunday afternoons, isn't it, Vic?"

"Awful," Victoria agreed, gazing at Gavin. "It's much nicer at your house, Zara."

"Well, I'm afraid you'll have to wait here until I come

back and fetch you," Gavin said. "The Mini will only hold four."

"Oh, now, Gavin, don't be stuffy," Zara said at once, petulantly. "What's the point in making two people wait instead of one?"

"And which one had you in mind?" he asked grimly. "Yourself, I suppose?"

"Don't be silly, I haven't got a coat. Besides, I have to go with Nat and Vic, they're my guests. You can take Poppy back in your car and Mrs H can drive us girls, and Miss Ruskin can wait here. She'll be quite all right under the porch," she added hastily as Gavin's brows drew down alarmingly.

"You know perfectly well your mother doesn't want Poppy to ride in my car," he said. Emma felt a surge of impatience. For heaven's sake, doesn't this family do anything but argue? She was tired of being discussed like an inanimate object.

"It's all right, I can walk home," she said. "I need some fresh air. And I'd like to see a bit of the countryside."

"No, you wait here and I'll come back for you," Gavin said, accepting the inevitable.

"There's no need—"

"I said, I'll come back for you. It's raining and it's colder than you think, and you don't know the way. Please don't argue!" he added wearily as she opened her mouth to protest again, and she shrugged and closed it again. Gavin seized Zara's arm and was hurrying her towards the car, and the others followed, keeping well enough back not to hear what he might be saying to her. Emma waited until they had gone, and then started to walk, as she had always intended to. She wasn't going to be told what to do, especially not by God's Gift to Women. It wasn't very far, and it was a straight road. It wasn't as if she could get lost.

Maddeningly, Gavin was right about the cold. Emma had

only been walking a few minutes when she realised it, and was sorry she had started to walk. It would have been better to stay in the church porch and be picked up. But no, she had to be pig-headed and prove that a Londoner was equal to a little weather and a few country lanes!

But a country village on a Sunday in the rain was about the deadliest place imaginable. Every house was shut up tight, and there wasn't a soul in sight, not so much as a dog or a passing car. In London the streets were never deserted in daylight; there was always somebody about. Now the rain was coming down harder, and she could have sworn the drops were wetter than London rain. She turned up her coat collar and looked about for shelter, but she was just leaving the village and there wasn't so much as a tree in the hedgerow. The clouds were heavy and dark, making it seem like late afternoon, and the country lane stretched before her uninvitingly, flanked by tall wet hedges which shut out the view. I hate the countryside, she thought fervently, and stuffing her wet hands in her pockets for warmth, trudged on.

There was no sign of Gavin. He ought to have got back to her by now, even driving at a normal speed. She thought wistfully of bright lights and a roaring fire − well, to be honest, even the flat in Muswell Hill with the radiator full up and the telly on would be heaven compared with this vista of wet useless fields under a wet dark sky. Still no Gavin. She bet he'd forgotten her. He was having cocktails or something and being purred over by those girls. Or maybe he'd decided to let her walk and teach her a lesson. Either way, she reckoned she was on her own. The road ahead of her was curving now in what she decided was the wrong direction. She remembered the road they had come by had not been straight, and she reckoned she would shorten her walk by a good bit if she were to cut across the fields instead of walking round two sides of them by the road. And if Gavin did come back for her and missed her, he'd know she must have taken a short cut.

Anyone living in London, she thought, with all those twisty streets, must have a good enough a sense of direction to cross a few plain, straightforward fields. There was a gate in the hedge to her left, and she saw a field beyond of short, rather thin grass, and another gate on the far side. Brilliant, she thought. No problem to a genius like me.

She was half way across when she heard someone shouting. She thought perhaps it was Gavin, and walked on, ignoring it loftily. The shouting was renewed, louder this time, and she realised belatedly it was not Gavin's voice.

"Hoi, you! What the hell d'you think you're doing? Stop right there!"

She looked round and saw a large man in gumboots hurrying round the edge of the field towards her. He was waving an angry fist, and under his other arm he carried what looked suspiciously like a gun.

"Trampling all over my young wheat, you bloody trespassing vandal! I'll have the law on you! Stand still, damn you!"

Only now did Emma see that where she had walked there was a dark track through the thin green vegetation. Oh dear, she thought, her face hot with shame: not grass after all. The man was coming closer. Under his flat cap his face was red and angry, and it was definitely a gun he was carrying. Was he allowed to shoot trespassers? And if not, did he know he wasn't? She didn't feel inclined to find out. She was close to the gate now, and going back would be as bad for his wheat as going on, she reasoned, so much better she avoid the confrontation. She ran for the gate, to renewed yelling from the man behind her, and scrambled over in frantic haste, glad she had always been agile. In the field beyond the grass looked like grass, but she was taking no chances – and besides, crossing the middle of the field she'd make too good a target. She turned aside and began running as fast as she could along the side of the field, keeping close to the hedge.

She couldn't see another gate, apart from the one she had

just come over, at which the man with the gun had now appeared and was inviting her to come back so that he could teach her to trample people's crops. Pass on that one, she thought. The hedge she was jogging beside was rather threadbare in places, especially at the bottom, and after a bit she came to a place where she judged it would be possible to squeeze through. She managed it, with a struggle and some damage to her appearance, and found herself in another field, which had a gate on the far side, through which she could see a road. Getting her bearings, she decided triumphantly it was the same road, and that she had definitely cut off a wide loop. All the same, she was now very wet, cold and dispirited, and would be extremely glad to get back to civilisation.

This grass really was grass, she decided, short and ragged and bitten down. Besides, there were cow-flops about, and that meant it couldn't be a crop, could it? Pleased with her powers of deduction she hunched her shoulders against the suddenly heavier rain, and hurried on.

Then she saw something move out of the corner of her eye. She looked, and through the mist of the driving rain she saw the black and white beasts gathered by the hedge, and realised the significance of the cow-dung. Well, cows were all right, she told herself firmly; cows didn't hurt you. She was not going to behave like someone out of a Carry On film and run away from cows thinking they were bulls. She might be a townie but she wasn't that green. She walked on steadily.

One of the creatures had left the others and was walking towards her. Its path would intersect hers just before she reached the gate. Why would one cow want to inspect her when the others didn't? She began to feel a little nervous. The cow hurried up a bit and got itself between her and the gate, and it stopped, turning a little so that she saw it sideways on for the first time. That was when she noticed that it didn't have an udder.

She turned cold, and stopped dead, frozen to the spot.

58

A cow without an udder couldn't be a cow. That meant it must be a bull. She was alone in a field miles from anywhere, with a bull between her and the only gate.

The bull stared at her, and tossed its head. Sizing up where to gore her, was her panicky thought. Oh, what a fool she'd been! Why hadn't she listened to Gavin? Why did she have to go and prove herself?

Mustn't run, she thought. Above all, mustn't make any sudden move. Keep calm, and keep still. It was just staring at her. Maybe if she inched away very slowly to the right she could get to the hedge and force her way through. Slowly does it. Slo-o-wly.

And then a small red car drew up in the road beyond the gate, and to her unmingled relief the familiar form of Gavin Akroyd stepped out and came up to the gate.

"What in blazes do you think you're doing?" he asked in his most supercilious, but at that moment welcome, voice. The bull looked round at him and then back at Emma, and moved a step away from him, which brought it closer to her.

"Don't shout!" she implored in a strangled voice. "Don't startle it. You'll make it charge me."

"Make it—? Oh, for heaven's sake!" In one fluid movement he vaulted over the gate, and the bull gave a snort and a sort of curtsy, and bounced away from both of them, pausing a little way off to turn and look at them again. Gavin ignored it and walked over to her, gripping her upper arms as he realised her legs were about to give way.

"What on earth are you doing, standing about in the middle of a field like a halfwit?" he asked her unamiably. "What are you doing in a field at all, for that matter? I thought I told you to wait in the church porch."

"You told me, yes – and then you didn't come," she retorted through clenched teeth. She was beginning to shiver uncontrollably, from cold or reaction, she didn't know which. "What was I supposed to think?"

"I'm sorry, I got held up. But you should have waited. You didn't think I'd just leave you there?"

Put like that, it did seem unlikely – and insulting to him, really, to suppose it. She muttered something ungracious.

"Come on, let's get you to the car. I'm surprised at you, being afraid of a mere cow."

Here it comes, she thought, the poor ignorant townie bit! "I'm not afraid of cows," she said shortly through her chattering teeth. "But any sane person is afraid of a bull – except, apparently, the great Gavin Akroyd."

"That wasn't a bull, you ignoramus," he said, amused.

She pulled her arm free from his grip and turned to face him angrily. "Now look here, don't try and get smart with me," she said, almost crying. "I know a bull from a cow when I see one! Cows have udders!"

He was grinning now, shaking his head with amusement. "Is that how you figured it out? You poor mutt, they're all heifers in this field. Maiden cows. Their udders haven't developed yet."

"Well, how the hell was I supposed to know that?" she shouted in a temper.

He lifted his hands as if to hold her off. "Pax! It's not my fault you decided to plunge into the Great Outback. Besides, even if your little friend there had charged you, she couldn't have done you much harm. They've all been de-horned."

Well, so they had, she saw now. Why hadn't she noticed that before? Her humiliation complete, she walked beside him in silence back to the car, not even comforted by the fact that he was managing quite creditably not to laugh. He let her in, went round the other side and climbed in beside her, and started the engine. "I'll put the heater full up," he said kindly. "You must be frozen, you poor thing."

It felt wonderfully warm inside the car, and the smell of new upholstery was comforting, essentially a smell of civilisation.

"Thanks," she said gruffly. He drove off, and she felt a

little remorseful. A puddle was gathering at her feet. "I'm making a mess of your nice clean car," she said in a small voice. "I'm sorry."

"Don't worry about it," he said. For some reason, she saw, glancing at his profile, he seemed to be enjoying the situation. "When we get back, you'd better go straight upstairs and have a hot bath. You don't want Zara's chums seeing you like that."

Now that was sheer kindness. She looked at him in surprise, and saw a smile directed towards her so different from anything she had seen on his face before that it made her insides turn over.

"Thanks," she said. She felt confused. Something was happening here, she thought; some contact was being made between them which she had not at all expected. She knew nothing about him, and yet she could feel herself liking him, as if they had known each other a long time; and him liking her, which was even more odd and unlikely. "Um, look—" she began hesitantly.

"Yes?"

"About that cow—?"

Now he was positively grinning. "I won't tell a soul," he pledged. His eyes met hers, full of warmth and, the last thing she expected to see, some uncertainty. "But on one condition," he added.

"Which is?"

"That you take the job as Poppy's governess."

She hesitated. "I haven't been offered it yet."

"You will be."

"How can you be sure?"

"I'm sure. Look here, Poppy likes you – she told me so – and she doesn't like many people. And I think you'll be right for her. So will you take the job? Please?"

Afterwards, she was always sure it was that 'please' that decided her. It seemed so unlike him, and she was a sucker for novelty.

61

Chapter Six

Since Emma was available, there seemed no reason not to start her trial period at once; so on Monday she went back to London to pack up her belongings. Gavin said he would be in London himself that afternoon, and to her surprise he offered to pick her and her luggage up at the flat and drive her back. She was pleased, not only because it would save humping cases to the railway station, but also because she'd be able to show him off to her flatmates. And then she caught herself up sharply. Show him off? He was her potential future employer's son, that was all!

Atkins drove her to the station for the earliest train. "I'm glad you're coming back," he said. "Makes one more human being in the house. Score one to our side, eh?"

"After the reception I got the first evening, I was surprised they wanted me," Emma said.

He glanced at her. "Did their best to put you off, did they? But the Guv'nor's all right, his bark's worse than his bite. Her ladyship don't like nobody, that's a cross we all have to bear. And Zara's a spoilt little cow that wants smacking, that's all. Don't let 'er bother you none."

Emma didn't say anything, but she felt embarrassed. Ought they to be discussing the family behind their backs, especially in these terms? If she agreed with him, would her words get back to her potential employers?

He seemed to understand her thoughts. "Don't worry, I wouldn't say nothing. Had a go at you, did she? Her trouble is, she's jealous of everybody and everything. Keep an eye on her, is my advice. She'd stab you in the back as soon as look at you."

She thought she might as well get the full low-down while she could. "What do you think of Gavin?" she asked.

"He's a bit of a stuffed shirt, but he can't help that. That was the way he was brought up. And he's had females buzzing around him all his life, so he can't help thinking he's God's gift. I've known a score of young ladies mad about him, but he's never cared a jot for anyone but himself, as far as I can see – and why should he? He don't need anybody. He's straight enough with me, that's all I care about; but then I've known him since he was a kid. He knows he'd get short shrift if he give me any of the old acid."

This was not encouraging, though it was what Emma had suspected about him. "He was the first Mrs Akroyd's son, wasn't he?"

"That's right." He glanced at her again, to gauge her interest. "She wasn't a nob any more than the Guv'nor. Childhood sweethearts, they were. Lived next door to each other when they was kids. Nice woman, she was, too – no nonsense about her. She doted on Gavin. But then when Mr A started to get rich, nothing would do for him but Gavin had to go to public school and mix with other rich kids. So they packed him off to some posh boarding school. It nearly broke his mum's heart, but she wanted the best for him so she went along with it. Then while he was away at school, she died. He was only nine."

"Oh, I am sorry! Was he very much upset?"

"Bound to've been, I should think; but he never shows his feelings much. I reckon that's what made him so stiff and stand-offish, anyway; especially when his dad married Lady Susan so soon after. You know what kids are like."

"I suppose he'd see it as a betrayal of his mother."

"Yeah. Well, it stands to reason he must've known his mum was only a common woman, dunnit?"

"But surely nobody minds about that sort of thing any more," Emma protested.

"Don't they?" he snorted. Emma thought about the first evening and realised she was dealing with a different kind of world now. "Well, him and Lady Susan have never got on, though they're always polite to each other, of course. And there's no love lost between him and Zara. He likes the twins all right, but they're away at school most of the time. And Poppy—"

Just at that interesting moment they pulled up at the station entrance, and Atkins interrupted himself to say, "'Ow about that for timing? That's your train coming in now! Better step on it – they don't hang about for passengers these days. Got your ticket?"

"Yes, thanks." Emma gathered her bags. "Thanks very much for the lift."

"S'my job, ennit? Be seeing you, then."

"Yes, very soon." .

"I knew it! They've thrown her out! She's come back to us!" Suzanne cried as she opened the door to Emma.

"Well, yes and no," Emma smiled, pushing past her. "I smell something cooking! I'm starving."

"What, they didn't even feed you? The way the rich treat their servants is shameful," Suzanne pretended indignation.

"Is that you, Em?" Alison said, coming out from the sitting-room. "You're early. Chucked you out, have they?"

"What's that?" Rachel appeared from the kitchen. "They did what? Oh, poor Emma!"

"You're all very eager for me to fail my first job inter-view," Emma complained. "But I might as well put you all out of your misery. They liked me, I'm on a month's trial, and I've just come back for my things."

"Well, congratulations," Rachel said. "Come into the

kitchen and tell us everything. I've got a cake in the oven. It should be ready any minute."

"Are they filthy rich?" Alison asked.

"Strinking," Emma said, sitting down at the kitchen table and easing off her shoes. "Oh, this is comfortable!"

"Tired of the high life already?" Suzanne asked with a cynical smile. "What's the house like?"

"Rambling and Tudor. They only live in one wing. It stands in a huge park – a mile from the gate to the house, just like in all the stories – and they've so many servants I haven't counted them all yet."

"Fantastic!" Alison said.

"I suppose you have to live in the servants' hall and sleep in an attic?" Suzanne said.

"No, I shall have my own room and bathroom, and I'm supposed to be one of the family, but as far as possible I mean to have my meals with Poppy – that's the little girl's nickname. Oh, thanks," she added as Rachel put a mug of tea in front of her.

"Why the segregation?" Suzanne asked. "Didn't you like them?"

Emma frowned. "They're not a happy family. Mr Akroyd's a bit of a rough diamond. 'I'm a plain man and I know what I like': that sort of thing. But I don't think there's any real harm in him, and he'll be away a lot anyway. There are two little boys I haven't seen yet, but they're away at school most of the time. Lady Susan's as cold as charity, hardly speaks and never looks at you. And Zara, the elder girl, has got a chip on her shoulder, is rude and sullen, and has taken an instant dislike to me."

"How lovely for you!" Suzanne said. "Just what you need to make you feel at home."

"Poor Emma, isn't there anyone nice there?" Rachel said, getting her cake out of the oven.

"Poppy seems like a nice little thing, but rather nervous and down-trodden. She's been though some kind of emotional trauma and she's got a food-phobia – hardly eats a thing – but she seems to want to be friendly, which is the main thing."

"It's not what I'd call the main thing," Alison said. "What're you going to do for a social life?"

"Oh, I might be able to get the occasional game of darts in the village pub," Emma said airily.

"You can't bury yourself in the country like that," Alison said, looking shocked. "How are you going to meet any men?"

"I'll come up to London on my days off and you can line them up for me," Emma said.

"Oh well, it's only for a month, anyway," Suzanne said firmly.

Emma laughed. "That's my girl! Never look on the bright side! That cake smells heavenly, Rache. I suppose there's no chance of a piece for a starving traveller?"

"Of course. I don't mind cutting it now. Or would you like something more substantial?"

"No, thanks all the same, just a piece of cake. I haven't got long. I've got to get my things together. Gavin's calling for me in about an hour."

There was a brief silence, and then the three of them said with one voice, "Who's Gavin?"

"Oh, didn't I mention Gavin?"

"No, you didn't," Rachel said.

"Now I wonder why the omission?" Alison added with heavy irony. "A bit of a Freudian slip, that. Significant, wouldn't you say?"

"Not a bit. He's the son of the house. Late twenties. Very superior."

"In what way?" Suzanne asked suspiciously.

"Aloof and proud," Emma said.

Alison and Rachel exchanged a look, and Alison sighed. "Pity. I thought for a minute—"

"Not for the fraction of a minute," Emma said warningly.

It was comfortable to be back at the flat, to be able to wander round barefoot and not be on one's best behaviour, to be able to say what one liked without being afraid of being misunderstood or snubbed. Home, however shabby, certainly had its advantages. She was almost sorry when the doorbell rang to announce Gavin's arrival – almost, but not quite. It was going to be an adventure, and she was ready for an adventure.

The other three had been watching the afternoon film in the sitting-room. "I'll get it!" Suzanne yelled, and beat Alison off the mark. By the time Emma got into the hall, Suzanne was gone, the flat door was standing open, and the other two were standing about expectantly.

"She's gone down to the street door," Rachel said. "Maybe it got stuck again."

"Or maybe your Gavin doesn't understand about buzzers. P'raps the upper classes don't have them," said Ali.

"I hope you're not going to shame me and make embarrassing remarks like that in front of him," Emma said severely. "Look, come into the sitting-room, for heaven's sake. You can't stand about here like a WI committee."

They followed her reluctantly and seated themselves, watching the sitting-room door like children waiting for the conjurer. And when Suzanne appeared, her cheeks unexpectedly pink, she behaved like the conjurer, almost waving him in as she announced largely, "Girls, let me introduce Gavin Akroyd!"

She stepped aside, and Gavin filled the doorway. Even Emma, prepared for his amazing good looks, was stunned by the sight of him – for he was *smiling*! Not just a small, polite quirk of the lips, either, but a full, open and friendly smile. It made him look even more handsome; she wondered he didn't know that, and make more use of it.

"Now, let me introduce everyone," Suzanne said quickly, with a proprietorial air, as though afraid someone else might get there first. "This is Alison — she works at Sartoriana, d'you know it? In Bond Street. Yes, I thought you might. And this is Rachel — she's a teacher." By the tone of her voice, she might just as well have said 'She's *only* a teacher.' "And this is Emma — oh, silly of me, of course you know Emma."

"Not as well as I hope to," Gavin said, which effectively silenced her for the next ten minutes. He said hello to the others, and went on, "I hope I'm not barging in on you. I expect this kind of thing is a bit of a nuisance. What's the film like, any good?"

He was all pleasant smiles as he advanced into the room, looking as though he only wanted an invitation to sit down and take his shoes off with the rest of them. Suzanne and Alison both answered at once, clashed and stopped each other, and Rachel filled the gap by saying, "Can I offer you a cup of tea, Mr Akroyd? I was just going to make one."

"Oh, Gavin, please. Yes, I'd love one, if it's no trouble."

He sat down on the sofa. Rachel went to put the kettle on, and the other two sat down nearby, perched well forward on their seats, and fixed him with eager expressions.

"I was just telling Gavin that my firm did the decorations for his house," Suzanne said, getting the name off with telling ease.

"It was a very nice job, from what Mrs Henderson told me," Gavin said. "She's the housekeeper. It's mostly her and Dad who use the London house. I haven't seen it, actually, since it's been done."

"Nor has Suzanne," Alison said nastily.

"No, but I've seen the plans and the samples," Suzanne said, colouring. "You live in the country, then?" she asked Gavin hastily, to cover her retreat.

"When I'm home. I'm away a lot, though not as much as Dad."

"What do you do?" Alison asked. "I suppose you're going to inherit the family business?"

Emma frowned at her, thinking it sounded rude, but Gavin didn't seem upset.

"Yes, but that sounds a bit feudal. I didn't want to take a seat on the Board without knowing anything about the business, so when I finished at university I went and worked for a time at each of the plants, to get to know the processes from the ground up. And then I went on a management training course, partly here and partly in Brussels. Dad didn't like the idea, but I told him someone had to understand what was going on in Europe, and he said in that case it had better be me. He hates the whole idea of Europe."

Emma couldn't get over the difference in him. Before long Suzanne and Alison were sitting back and relaxing, and conversation was flowing easily. Rachel brought in tea and the remains of her cake, and they all chatted about such diverse subjects as films, restaurants, the merits of streaming in schools, whether mugs were preferable to cups, rail privatisation, and which cars gave the best performance on country roads.

Emma joined in very little, preferring to listen and observe. There wasn't a hint of coldness or stiffness about him. What had wrought the miracle? Could it be that he felt at ease here, whereas at home he felt constrained? Or was he like this with everyone except her? Maybe she brought out the worst in him. Well, she had started off by mocking and teasing him; but then he'd started off by freezing and snubbing her. Perhaps they were doomed to rub each other up the wrong way, she thought gloomily.

He seemed to have settled in for the duration, but she knew the contents of the communal larder, and didn't want the girls to have to ask him (and her) to stay and eat, so at last she interrupted. "Don't you think we ought to get going?"

For an instant Gavin actually looked disappointed; then he looked at his watch and his expression registered concern. "I didn't realise it was as late as that! Yes, we better had make a move."

"You must come again," Suzanne said quickly. "Any time you're passing."

"Yes, any time," Alison added. "No need to ring first – just drop in. You're always welcome."

Oi, what about me? Emma thought. Can I come again? But she was as moon to sun, as far as her friends were concerned, with Gavin Akroyd in the room.

They said prolonged goodbyes standing in the hall, and then at last Gavin picked up her bags and they were off. As they drove away along Muswell Hill Road, Gavin said quietly, "What fun it must be, living in a flat like that."

"I'm sorry?" Emma said, wondering if she had heard him right.

He hesitated, as if not sure whether to go on or not; and then he said, "I envy you, living in a flat like that. The freedom. The friendship. The good times you must have had."

"Well – yes," she said, thinking it an odd comment. Hadn't he had fun like that? "Surely you shared a flat when you were at university?"

"No," he said. "I stayed at home and commuted in. I went to Cambridge, you see."

"Oh. Nice," Emma said blankly.

He glanced sideways at her. "I went to Cambridge so that I *could* commute," he said. "With Dad away so much, he wanted me at home to take care of things."

"Oh, I see," said Emma. That seemed rather unfair, denying him the usual student jollies, putting responsibility on him so young. "But I suppose it was nice for you to be at home, in a way," she said, "with your brothers and sisters."

He didn't answer at once, and then he said, "I'm very fond of Poppy."

"She's a very sweet kid," Emma answered at once; but

70

reflected afterwards that his comment had been remarkable for what it didn't say. She thought of Atkins's words: *Him and Lady Susan have never got on* and *There's no love lost between him and Zara.* To be made perpetually responsible for a family you didn't like must have been a burden indeed. She felt sorry for him.

"Tell me about your family," he said after a bit; and there was nothing she was happier doing. The atmosphere grew warmer and more lively. When she had told him something of her life, she slipped in a question or two about his. He told her about his love of the countryside: described solitary walks along the beach at Aldeburgh; birdwatching at Dunwich; sitting up all night in the forest watching for badgers; riding through the deep Suffolk lanes; sailing on the Orwell; hunting on crisp winter mornings. Through his words she was transported to a world so different from hers in London that it sounded like an Arthurian legend, a magical place of improbable beauty.

"God, you're so lucky!" she said at last. "How can you possibly envy me? It's me who should envy you!"

"How can you say that?" he asked, the light in his eyes fading a little. "What can you envy about my life?"

She felt this was going a little far. "Come," she said crisply, "you've had every advantage money could buy."

"Oh, money," he said. "Yes, I had that."

"It's all very well sneering at it," she said, feeling a little cross. "You can afford to say money doesn't matter as long as you've got enough of it. Privilege is easy to belittle when you've got it."

"Yes, I am privileged," he said. "But you've had a different sort of privilege, and one that I'd have been happy to swap mine for. But I don't suppose you'd believe me if I told you so."

"No, not for a minute," she said. She tried to say it lightly, teasingly, but he didn't smile.

"At least you can be sure that when people say they like

you, it's you they like," he said in a low voice, almost too low for her to hear.

"What do you mean by that?" she asked.

"Oh, nothing," Gavin said, and he sounded quite depressed.

The change seemed to start then. The animation left his face, and he said nothing more. Emma, looking at his non-committal profile, wondered whether he was thinking of Zara's girl-friends throwing themselves at him. We should all have his problems! she thought. She couldn't help feeling that being spoilt for choice was better than having Hobson's choice, and that the anxieties of having too much money must be easier to bear than those which came with having too little.

The rest of the journey was accomplished in almost complete silence. Emma would have liked to chat, but somehow she couldn't find the right words to begin. When she did broach a subject, he answered her too briefly to get the conversation going again, and after a few such snubs she gave up. His aloofness, or grimness, whichever it was, seemed to intensify the nearer they got to Long Hempdon. What a Jekyll and Hyde character he was turning out to be, she thought to herself. Was it the proximity to home that affected him so adversely, or was it her? He had been so relaxed and easy at the flat, but now after a period alone with her, he had gone back to his usual withdrawn and chilly manner.

Oh well, whatever the cause, she told herself with a shake, it hardly mattered. Her duties were with the little girl, Poppy, and she didn't particularly have to get on with Poppy's big brother. She would be unlikely to see much of him, spending most of her time in the schoolroom and nursery; and in any case, hadn't he said that he was away a lot? No, Mr Gavin Akroyd was not likely to have much effect on her day-to-day life – and that was probably just as well, she thought, glancing briefly at that icy, uncommunicative profile.

Chapter Seven

It was one of those glorious early summer days in May, and the soft air coming in through the open window of the day-nursery (now the schoolroom) was sweet with the scents of grass and flowers. It was hard to concentrate on lessons, even for Emma, so she could hardly blame Poppy for fidgeting and staring out of the window when she should have had her mind on arithmetic. Both pairs of eyes seemed to be inexorably drawn to the brightness outside every few minutes. They usually took a break at half past ten, but at a few minutes past the hour Emma decided to bow to the inevitable.

"I think we'll take our break now – what do you think?" she said, closing the book. "Shall we stop or go on? It's a bit early, but—"

Poppy shut her own book smartly and beamed with relief. "Oh yes! Break, please."

"Perhaps we can take our elevenses outside. It's such a lovely day. Have you got another favourite spot you'd like to show me?"

As far as possible, Emma had been letting Poppy show her round the house and grounds, a small act of empowerment that she felt the little girl badly needed. In the time she had been here, Emma had discovered a great deal she didn't like very much about Poppy's situation. The Akroyd family was what she had learned at teacher-training college to call dysfunctional; the members seemed to perform their own separate orbits, entirely detached from each other, never intersecting. Mr Akroyd was away a good deal, and when he was at home was usually shut up in his study haranguing someone on the telephone. When he was with his family, his temper seemed on a very short fuse, and when he went away again, Emma couldn't help feeling relieved.

Lady Susan led an even more mysterious life, in the sense that Emma had no idea what she did with herself all day. Sometimes she went out in the car, driven by Atkins, shopping, or to visit friends; less frequently a friend visited her for lunch or tea. When Emma met her about the house, she drifted past without looking at her. She didn't seem to interest herself in Poppy at all, and certainly never came near the schoolroom. Perhaps she didn't care for so many stairs, Emma thought to herself with grim humour.

Gavin she found very difficult to fathom. She didn't have much to do with him, and when she came upon him unexpectedly in the house, he was usually cool and aloof, merely nodding to her or greeting her formally. At dinner he rarely spoke; but just once or twice, in the drawing-room after dinner, when his father had been called away to the telephone, Zara was out about her own amusements, and Mrs Henderson was occupied with keeping Lady Susan from the tedium of her own company, Gavin had seated himself beside Emma and engaged her in conversation. And it had been pleasant, stimulating, and had given her a glimpse of a hidden person she felt she would have liked to get to know better. But it never lasted long. The next time she saw him he would be distant with her again, as though trying to backtrack on any advance in intimacy she might presume upon. She always felt that he was very aware of her status as an employee in the house, and kept her at arm's length because of it. He would talk to her for as long as it amused him, and then drop her. That was the way, she supposed, he was with women. After Chris, it didn't surprise her.

And yet he interested her. He seemed so much the odd one out of the family; and Poppy spoke of him with such wistful affection. If Poppy liked him, Emma thought, he couldn't be all bad. And she was aware that, little as they had to do with each other, there was something about her that interested him. Often she would catch him looking at her, during those silent dinners; his gaze would be hastily withdrawn as soon as she looked up. But she couldn't flatter herself it was the interest of approval; a fascination of loathing was just as likely.

She had made the brief acquaintance of the twins Harry and Jack in their short time at home between their Easter skiing holiday and their return to school. They were tall, handsome boys with cut-glass accents; beautifully dressed, and with beautiful manners and more self-possession than seemed natural in fourteen-year-olds. All the other boys of that age Emma had ever known were at their most awkward, by turns shy and surly, childish and aggressive; greasy, spotty, violently untidy, strangers to the bathroom and unable to carry on a normal conversation with anyone but their own compadres. Harry and Jack were so unlike this template Emma found it hard to believe they were human.

The difference their presence made to their mother was the greatest revelation to Emma. For a few short days, Lady Susan became animated. She beamed, she attended, she asked questions and listened to the answers. She evidently doted on the boys, and if they were not dancing attendance on her she pursued them to their haunts, forever wanting to touch them, and seeming riveted by their slightest utterance. The boys took this in good part, but in the opportunities she had to observe them she could not see that they felt any great affection for their parent in return. They bore with her because they were too polite not to, but they were glad to get away from her.

They were polite to Emma, too, with that delightful courtesy of well-brought-up children towards those they hold in utter indifference. They lived only for each other, and had elevated the skills of escaping to be alone together into an art-form. Emma felt very sorry for Poppy, who was even more eclipsed by their sudden glamour; and could not help noticing how differently Lady Susan behaved towards them as opposed to Poppy. Emma supposed she was one of those women who only cared for their sons and thought their daughters nothing. Poppy would have liked to be with the twins, join their conversations and go with them on their jaunts; but they would not have her. They were kind to her in an off-hand way, but they did not want her company.

When the boys went back to school, Zara did too, for her last term. Emma was glad to have her out of the house, since she was invariably rude and contemptuous and had many small ways of making Emma's life uncomfortable. Emma wondered how she would manage when Zara came back for good: there was no prospect of her going to university, it seemed, and in fact her present school was of the finishing rather than the academic variety. She supposed Zara would be launched into society and lead the same kind of life as her mother. Emma hoped she would be able to inculcate some harder ambition in Poppy's breast than being a clothes-horse and getting married. She could only assume that was what she had been hired for, though she sometimes wondered whether it wasn't just to keep the child out of her mother's way.

At the very least, though, she could give Poppy someone of her own to pay attention to her and offer her affection. The isolation in which the child had led most of her life so far seemed terrifying to Emma.

Now, in answer to Emma's question, Poppy said eagerly, "Can we go down to the kitchen? Mrs Grainger said she was making Chelsea buns this morning and they'd be ready for elevenses."

"Did she indeed? I love buns."

"Me too! They're the best!" Poppy said eagerly, relief flooding her face that she was not to be denied the treat.

"She won't mind our going down there?"

"No, she likes it. Really," Poppy said earnestly.

"OK then, let's go."

It was the first time Emma had been 'below stairs', and she was intrigued when Poppy led her into a part of the house she had not seen before, through a concealed door which looked like part of the corridor wall, and down what were evidently the backstairs. They were of bare wood, uncarpeted and dusty, but the smell of food drifted up them like a friendly ghost. Poppy pattered down with evident familiarity, all the way from the top to the bottom of the house, emerging into a dim, flagstoned corridor lined with panelled cupboards, and pushing through another door into the kitchen.

It was warm and full of the smell of baking; sunlight streamed in through a high window. The walls were of rough whitewashed stone and the floor stone-flagged, wavy with centuries of footsteps. There was a large old-fashioned deal table, and an ancient built-in pine dresser, but other-wise everything was modern: strip-lights in the ceiling, modern cupboards and units, a huge steel industrial cooking-stove, racks of stainless steel pots and pans overhead, an enormous dishwasher and a big American-style larder-fridge the size of a wardrobe. Under the vast Tudor chimney a four-oven Aga looked almost lost, and in front of it Mrs Grainger was sitting with her feet up on a stool, having a cup of tea and reading the *Daily Mirror*.

She looked up and smiled as they came in. "Ah, there you are. Let you off, has she?" she said to Poppy.

"You did say," Poppy answered defensively, out of her chronic anxiety.

"I did say," Mrs Grainger agreed economically.

"I hope we aren't disturbing you?" Emma put in.

"Not a bit. I was hoping to meet you, and I knew They'd never bring you down. So I told Poppy I'd make some buns." She nodded towards the Aga, on top of which the promised

77

Chelsea buns were cooling on a wire rack. "Can I offer you a cup of tea, Miss Ruskin?"

"Emma, please. Yes, I'd love one, thank you."

"Me too?" Poppy pleaded.

Mrs Grainger looked sidelong at Emma. "You're supposed to have milk. It's better for you."

"I don't like milk. Please can't I have tea, Emma? I always do down here."

"Tattle-tail, giving me away!" Mrs Grainger chided her.

Emma thought of her own childhood home, where everyone drank strong orange tea from babyhood upwards. It never did them any harm. "I won't tell. And tea is supposed to be good for the heart, now, isn't it?"

"Is it? They're always changing the rules, aren't they?" Mrs Grainger said placidly, pouring the tea. Poppy and Emma pulled up chairs, and the buns were transferred to a plate and dredged with sugar. They were soft, fragrant, sticky, bursting with fruit, and more delicious than anything Emma had ever tasted before. Shop buns were the palest, feeblest imitation beside them, and Emma said so.

"I'm glad you like them," Mrs Grainger said, looking pleased. "I really enjoy baking, you've always got something to show at the end of it. Yeast baking especially. But I get precious little chance these days, unless the boys are home. Mr Akroyd likes his cake hearty, but he's never here; and her ladyship only wants the dainty stuff if she has afternoon tea."

"Well count me in, any time you've got buns to get rid of," Emma said. "This is sheer heaven."

"And how are you settling in? Finding your way around all right?"

"Yes, thank you. Poppy's showing me everything, bit by bit."

"I was hoping to get to see you. I said to Bill to ask you to come down for tea some time—"

"Bill?"

"Bill Atkins, the chauffeur."

"Oh yes. Sorry, I didn't know his first name."

Poppy finished her first bun and asked if she could have another. "Yes, as long as you don't spoil your lunch," Mrs Grainger said. Poppy took another and began nibbling it in a circle, unrolling it as she went. "Take it with you and go and see the kittens, why don't you?" the cook suggested beguilingly.

"Can I? Are they still in the boot room?"

"Yes, but watch you don't let them out. And mind Tigger doesn't scratch you."

Poppy disappeared, bun in hand, through another door. Mrs Grainger turned to Emma. "I didn't want to talk about her while she was listening, but I wanted to say how much better she's been since you've come. There was a time I was really worried about her. She would hardly eat a thing except sweets, and it was making her ill."

"She's still very thin," Emma said.

"Yes, but Anna and Julie tell me she's eating much better now. They always keep an eye on her plate for me and report back. She's been a very unhappy child, you see."

"I understand she was at school for a while."

"Yes, but she didn't fit in there. The other girls teased her, and the teachers didn't stop it. Anyway, Poppy got really unhappy and even tried running away, but her dad gave her a lecture and said she'd got to stay, so she just went into a decline and made herself ill. Came back at the end of term like a shadow, and then Jean Henderson stepped in and said enough was enough and persuaded Gavin to make Mr Akroyd to let her stay home."

"Gavin?"

Mrs Grainger looked at her, eyebrows raised. "Oh yes, he loves that kid. Ever since she was born, he's doted on her. He's practically like a father to her, and she worships the ground he walks on, as I expect you know. Trouble is, he's got so much else to do, he hasn't got the time to spend with her. And he's been away from home so much in the past couple of years, he hasn't been able to keep an eye on her."

"I'm surprised," Emma said. "I mean, I'm very pleased that she has someone who cares for her, but I wouldn't have thought Gavin would be the type to—" She paused, not wishing to offend.

"Oh, there's a lot of good in that young man," Mrs Grainger said. "I know he can seem stand-offish, but he's had a lot to put up with one way and another, and he's very shy, though you mightn't think it." Emma didn't. "Harry and Jack are all charm and easy manners, but Gavin's more serious-minded. He can't just be social like them."

"I suppose they learn that at public school."

"That's part of it. Oh, I'm no snob, I think Eton does them a lot of good. It's a pity Gavin never had the chance to go there. He went to boarding school, but it was quite a different sort of place; but then Mr A didn't know what he knows now. He hadn't married into the nobility then. You know Gavin was the son of Mr Akroyd's first wife? Yes, well, there's always been a lot of family tension. Her ladyship hasn't got any time for him, despite the fact that it's him that keeps everything together – the estate and everything. But of course she resents the fact that it will all go to him and not one of her own boys." She looked at Emma defensively. "I suppose I'm speaking out of turn a bit, but you'll find out for yourself sooner or later. And of course he's got no respect for her, especially over the way she's treated Poppy – or not treated her, really."

"It seems a very unhappy household, one way and another," Emma commented. "I wonder he doesn't leave – set up on his own somewhere."

"I expect he would have, if it hadn't been for Poppy. He doesn't trust anyone else to look after her. He doesn't want her growing up like Zara, you see – wants her to

80

get exams and have a career and everything, so she can be independent."

Emma decided to satisfy her curiosity on another subject. "Tell me, why does Zara dislike me? As far as I know, I haven't given her any reason to."

"Zara?" Mrs Grainger smiled at her. "Oh, that's easy! I should have thought you'd have realised—"

At that interesting moment the kitchen door from the main part of the house opened and Mrs Grainger broke off abruptly. It was Gavin.

"Mrs Grainger, have you seen Poppy?" he began, and then saw Emma, and frowned. It seemed, she thought resignedly, his natural reaction to her "Ah, Miss Ruskin. You're here, are you?" His voice sounded cool and disapproving. "I was wondering where you were. I went up to the schoolroom, expecting to find you there, but of course it was empty."

Checking up on me, she thought indignantly. She stood up. "We were having our morning break, Mr Akroyd," she said with dignity, "but I was just about to go back. Poppy's through there looking at the kittens."

Gavin's face seemed to flush slightly – with anger, Emma decided. "Don't let me drive you away," he said. "I'm surprised to see you here, but what you do during your break is your own affair."

She thought he was being sarcastic. "Our break is over, Mr Akroyd," she said stiffly. "It's time we got back to work. Thank you for the tea, Mrs Grainger." And without waiting for any further comment she made her escape, bristling indignantly, through the door Poppy had taken before her.

She always had breakfast, lunch and tea with Poppy in the day nursery, but dinner was taken with the family. It wasn't a very cheery meal, but at least she got to chat to Mrs Henderson, who could usually be relied on to be sociable.

On this particular evening Mr Akroyd was absent, and Gavin took his place at the end of the table. Lady Susan

81

was silent as usual until about half way through the meal, when she suddenly laid down her fork and addressed Emma out of the blue, cutting across a rather rambling account Mrs Henderson was giving of some alterations to the gardens.

"I understand that you took Arabella down to the kitchen this morning."

Emma looked at her, surprised, and just managed not to say, "What, me?" Instead she said, "Yes, that's right."

"I should be glad, Miss Ruskin," Lady Susan said with something approaching animation, "if you would never do such a thing again." Her eyes were fixed on a spot somewhere beyond Emma's left shoulder. Emma felt her blood rise. Out of the corner of her eye she could see Gavin eating steadily with his head bent over his plate, his whole attitude redolent of guilt. Oh, I see, so that's what this is about, she thought. Sneak! Tell tale! Getting his mother to do his dirty work, is he?

"May I ask why?" Emma asked, her voice rising a little with resentment.

Lady Susan's eyes brows went up. Clearly she was not used to being questioned. "Because I don't wish her to be there. She is too fond of associating with the servants as it is. She must not be encouraged by you. That is all."

Emma had never heard anything so archaic. "I see. You think she'll be corrupted, or pick up bad habits, I suppose?"

Lady Susan was so astonished at Emma's answering back that she actually looked directly at her for an instant. But she spoke in the same, languid tone as always. "I will not be questioned in this way, Miss Ruskin. You will adhere to the rules I lay down concerning my daughter's upbringing, or you will seek another position."

Emma opened her mouth to say she would do just that, when she caught Mrs Henderson's anxious eye across the table. The housekeeper gave her a pleading look and a little shake of the head; and Emma thought of Poppy, and how the little girl needed her, and knew she must not sacrifice her for the sake of her own temper. So she swallowed her retort and bent her head to her plate instead, and forked in some food to prevent herself from speaking.

In the silence she heard Gavin clear his throat, but it was Mrs Henderson who spoke, reverting to the broken topic of gardens, and so the meal passed on.

As they were walking out from the dining-room later, Mrs Henderson said to Emma with an attempt at cheerfulness, "What are you going to do this evening?"

Get out of this house for a bit, at the very least, Emma thought; but she phrased it more politely. "Oh, I thought I'd go out for a walk, see a bit of the neighbourhood. I haven't set foot outside the park since I arrived here."

"What a good idea," Mrs Henderson said. "Are you heading anywhere in particular?"

Emma hadn't actually thought, but she said now, more or less at random, "I think I'll go down to the village and have a drink at the pub."

She hadn't realised Gavin was right behind her until he said, before Mrs Henderson could speak, "I'd rather you didn't do that."

It was the wrong way to put it, for the mood Emma was in. She turned, bristling. "And why not, may I ask?"

His face was grave. "It's not a very nice place," he said.

"Not very nice?" she repeated coldly. Like the kitchen, she supposed.

"It's rough. It's not suitable for someone like you."

Contamination of members of the household by the lower classes: that's what he was afraid of, the beastly snob! "You forget," she said, poison-sweet, "that I come from Hoxton. I expect it will seem nice enough to me."

"I doubt it," he said coldly. "Anyway, I would prefer you not to go anywhere near it." He said 'prefer', but the tone was a tone of command.

"Really, my dear," Mrs Henderson jumped in as Emma

drew breath to answer, "I think perhaps you'd better give the pub a miss. I tell you what, why not stay in tonight, and tomorrow evening early, go in to Cambridge on the train? You could go to the theatre or a movie and have supper there – there are some nice restaurants and bistros. Much more suitable."

Emma didn't want to have a row with Mrs Henderson, who was only trying to keep the peace, so she just said, "Very well," and left them, going up to her room. But inwardly she was seething. Did they think they owned her body and soul, just because they paid her wages? They didn't want their precious child's governess mixing with the lower classes – or their precious child mixing with servants, either. Really, these people! What world did they live in? Then she caught sight of her expression in the mirror, and laughed, her brow clearing. If she stayed here long she'd become as left-wing as Suzanne!

All the same, she wasn't going to be dictated to. If she wanted to go to the pub for a drink she'd go. She changed into slacks, put on her coat, took her handbag, and went out; down the backstairs to avoid bumping into anyone, and across the back hall. The evening was fine, and it was still light, and though it was a long walk into the village, she was glad to be out, and enjoyed the fresh air and the smells of grass and earth and evening dew.

By the time she reached the village, she was ready for a drink – and a sit down: country distances somehow seemed further than town ones. The pub, called the Dog and Duck, looked picturesque from a distance, a cob cottage with a thatched roof and crooked mullion windows, and there was a group of cheerful locals standing outside enjoying their evening ale *al fresco*. As she came closer, however, she found her enthusiasm waning a little. The place had a definite air of seediness about it: paint was falling off it in chunks, the thatch was infested with weeds, and the tarmac surrounding it was full of holes. Pop music

84

was blaring out of the open door, and the men standing outside were not genial, ruddy-faced farm lads off the set of a BBC costume drama, but a bunch of scruffy and extremely disagreeable-looking youths such as might be found hanging about any inner-city street corner – or, these days, the centre of any rural town.

They were watching her approach, and with the emptiness of the dark countryside behind her, she began to feel very exposed, and to realise how conspicuous she must look to them. The Dog and Duck did not look like the kind of pub a lone female would enter for fun; indeed, she wondered whether in this benighted place women ever went out alone. The youths were obviously talking about her, making remarks which she couldn't quite hear, but which made them laugh raucously amongst themselves.

Her footsteps slowed. Part of her wanted to turn tail and run, another part could not bear to be thwarted of her legitimate desires by a bunch of brainless yobs.

"'Ello, darlin', 'ow about a drink, then?" one of them called to her. She said nothing, but her heart sank, and her footsteps slowed still further.

"You out on your own?" another asked. "Ain't you scared, goin' about on yer own on a dark night like this?"

"Ne' mind, we'll look after yer, won't we?"

They all giggled and shoved each other, but their eyes were predatory.

"Well, say summink, can't yer? Wojjer want to drink, then?"

"She don't want to 'ave one wiv you – do yer, darlin'? She fancies me, dun't she. Come an' 'ave one wiv me."

"Nah, she don't mind – she'll 'ave one wiv all of us – won't yer, love?"

They roared with laughter at that, but they had drawn closer together and were now blocking the entrance to the pub, so that if she did want to go in, she would have to push past them, or ask them to move. Instinctively she knew

85

that in either case, they would not let her by, and physical jostling would follow, which was what they wanted. They were five and she was one, and they had absolute belief that they could do anything they wanted, and no-one could touch them for it.

But if she walked on past the pub, they might follow her. They must know by now that the pub was where she had been heading. If she walked by, they would know they had scared her, and would be elated by their power over her, and would certainly follow. And where else could she go? The few buildings nearby were in darkness. If they followed her into the darkness and caught her . . . She *must* go into the pub, even if it meant shoving past them, fighting her way in. Inside there would be a landlord and a telephone. It was her only chance of safety.

But while she had hesitated, they had grown in confidence. They were moving towards her now. They meant to keep her out of the pub, then. She began to feel really afraid. Would anyone inside hear if she screamed – or pay any attention if they heard? Would it make the yobs more or less likely to do her harm? She swallowed and licked her lips, searching for something to say to turn the situation, as they inched nearer, their eyes seeming to glitter like animals' eyes in the dark.

And then the sound of a car engine broke the tableau, the gutteral roar of a twin-exhaust sports car approaching at speed. The eyes flickered away from her for an instant; then headlights swung round the corner and washed over the pub façade, and the yobs ducked a little and put their hands up to shield their eyes from the dazzle. Emma turned, hardly daring to hope: but yes, it was Gavin's car, and it pulled up beside her with a squeal.

"Get in," he said tersely, leaning over to open the passenger-side door.

She didn't argue. She hurried round to the other side and got in, aware of the derisive hoots of the disappointed pack. Gavin barely waited for her to shut the door before gunning the engine, performing a tight and violent u-turn, and speeding away down the road. Emma was flung about, jerked backwards in her seat, and now had her hair blown forwards into her eyes.

"Do you have to drive like this?" she protested; but turning to look at him, she saw that he did. His lips were grimly closed, his nostrils taut and arching with fury. If he didn't take it out on the road, she thought, he'd probably take it out on her.

Then he did anyway. The words burst out of him like a major dam being breached. "What the hell do you think you're doing? I told you not to go to the pub! Did you think I was talking to myself?"

In the relief of being rescued, her own anger revived. "I don't see what business it is of yours where I go in my free time!" she retorted.

"Of course it's my business! In my father's absence I'm responsible for everybody in the house, even if it means protecting them from themselves! What d'you mean by prancing about the countryside in the dark like that? And going to the pub? Good God, Zara gives me worries enough, but even she knows better than that!"

This interesting reference passed Emma by in her fury. "I am not your sister, and I can take care of myself, thank you very much!"

"Oh, that's very evident! What did you intend doing about that gang of yobs? Wrestle them to the ground single-handed? I suppose you've got a black belt in karate you haven't told us about? Don't you know what would have happened if I hadn't turned up when I did?"

A slight tremble in his voice on the last words made her wonder if he had been really worried about her, as opposed to merely miffed that she had disobeyed him. Together with the realisation that he *had* rescued her from a horrid fate, it softened her a little.

"Look," she began in a more reasonable tone.

But he was not yet ready to be reasonable. "You were told not to go out. You were told the pub was rough. Yet you still went there. Are you stupid, or just infantile?"

Her anger flared again. "You *told* me, yes! You're very good at *telling* people what to do! You know all about what's suitable and what isn't. Maybe if you'd tried talking to me instead of issuing orders, I might not have assumed that it was just another example of your beastly snobbery!"

As soon as the words were out she trembled for her own rudeness – not that she cared if he sacked her, but she would be letting Poppy down. But instead of being furious, he seemed only surprised.

"Snobbery? But I'm not snobbish," he said in a voice that sounded genuinely puzzled.

"Not much, you're not!" she retorted. "You forbade Poppy from talking to Mrs Grainger, who's as kind a soul as I ever met, just because you didn't want a sister of yours mixing with servants!"

Her genuine grievance sounded clearly in her voice. Gavin threw a look sideways at her. "You don't think I had anything to do with that, do you? That was my stepmother's ban, not mine."

"But who put her up to it? You were the one who came in while we were there, and made it very clear you disapproved. You practically ordered me out of the kitchen."

To her surprise, Gavin stopped the car at the side of the road and turned to survey her thoughtfully. "No," he said quietly "you're quite wrong there. I wanted you to stay; I wanted to make conversation. But you were off like a scalded cat. I thought you disliked me so much you couldn't bear to be in the same room with me."

Emma was thrown off balance. "Then who—?"

"Who told my stepmother? I expect one of the maids mentioned it. But it was she who objected, not me, I assure you."

88

Emma couldn't think of a thing to say. He seemed to be taking pains to justify himself to her – and when she had just falsely accused him of an ignoble sentiment. He studied her face in the moonlight filtering through the trees at the side of the road, and she stared back defiantly, feeling herself weakening.

"So that's what all this was about?" he said at last. "You were punishing me by ignoring my advice about going out. Well, I honour the intention, if not the method. Will you shake hands and call a truce? I *was* right about the pub, wasn't I?"

"Yes," Emma said, and, determined to do the right thing if it killed her, she added, "I apologise for causing you trouble."

"I apologise too," he said.

"For what?"

In the dark he reached for her hand, and as his warm fingers closed round hers, the sensation made her start, and then almost tremble. He was very close to her in the confines of the car, and she felt his presence like a kind of radiation, as though she had come within the range of a great fire.

"For whatever I did to make you feel I wanted to drive you out of the kitchen. I assure you it was quite the opposite. I would have liked to talk to you, but—"

They looked at each other for a long moment, and Emma suddenly knew with absolute certainty that he was going to kiss her. The tension of the moment made all her nerve-endings tingle, and she found herself leaning towards him, everything inside her fluttering with anticipation. Her eyes began to close as his face came nearer, nearer; she could smell the fresh tang of his aftershave, and underneath it, the warm scent of his skin . . .

And then there was a roar, a blaze of light, the howl of a horn, and a car flashed past them at high speed, the headlight beams throwing the trees and hedges suddenly up into sharp relief, unreal, like a theatre backdrop. The wind of passing blatted briefly against the Elan, rocking it, and then swirled away with a scutter of leaves and grit as the car disappeared round the bend with a wag of its red tail-lights.

Gavin had dropped her hand, startled; and now did not reach for it again. The mood was broken. He re-started the car and drove on in silence. It was not exactly an unfriendly silence, but it was an awkward one. Emma could not think of anything to say to break it, and in the renewed tension she began to wonder if she had been mistaken in thinking he wanted to kiss her. That made her feel uneasy and embarrassed. She had made a big enough fool of herself over the pub; she didn't want to add to it by assuming more wrong and silly things about Gavin.

When they reached the house he stopped at the front to let her out, and she said quickly, "Well, thanks for the lift. Goodnight," and got out before he could say anything. She hurried up the steps, aware that he was sitting there watching her go. What was he thinking? Did he guess what she had expected and feel contempt for her because of it? Or had she just snubbed him again? She wondered what it was about Mr Gavin Akroyd, and whether she would ever manage to get her behaviour towards him right.

Chapter Eight

Over the next few days Emma found herself thinking more often than she was comfortable with about Gavin. Her mind continually strayed to the drive home, going over and over the words that were spoken, trying to recapture his tone of voice and expression. Most of all she kept thinking about that electrifying moment when she had been sure he was going to kiss her. Had it been pure imagination on her part? The more she thought about it the less she could be sure. Was it just wishful thinking? Maybe she had made a monumental fool of herself. Most likely he didn't think of her at all. She was just an employee, and a rather troublesome one at that.

But he *had* been worried about her. Surely that meant something? The tendency of her questions to herself made her realise that whatever his feelings, she was attracted to him. Maybe it was just because, shut up here in the house miles from anywhere, he was the only male within reach, and she had to be interested in somebody? Well, that was possible; but whatever the cause, she found herself looking forward more each day to the evening meal, the one time she might see him. Every evening she dressed herself with care, feeling that pleasant flutter of anticipation as she walked downstairs towards the drawing-room. And every evening there was the same disappointment. Gavin behaved towards her exactly as always, with calm, unemotional politeness. He joined in the conversation between her and Mrs Henderson, looked at her no more or less than before, called her, when he called her anything, Miss Ruskin. She might tell herself that there was a little more warmth in his eyes than before, but she could not be sure.

And really, she was glad not to be sure. It gave a spice to her days which was otherwise lacking. If she was sure he did not care for her at all, life would have been dull; but if she was sure he was interested in her, it would have meant she'd have to make up her mind about how she felt about him, and after Chris, she wasn't sure she wanted to.

But her preoccupation with the subject lasted only a few days; for after that Zara came home, and it was necessary to be careful to reveal nothing to the sharp eyes of disdain and jealousy: Zara would have been only too glad to make her life a misery if she thought for a moment Emma had dared to fancy her brother. And beside, Zara's return home shortly preceded her eighteenth birthday, for which there was to be a huge coming-of-age celebration. It was to be the grandest of grand affairs – both Mr Akroyd and Lady Susan, for different reasons, were determined on that. There was to be a ball to which most of the county would be invited, a vast buffet laid on by caterers, stewards and waitresses specially hired, champagne by the lakeful, and a cake of architectural proportions and elaboration.

Mrs Henderson told her more about it one afternoon, coming up to the schoolroom just after the end of lesson hours.

"It all sounds wonderful," Emma said. "Zara's a lucky girl. Is there anything I can do to help?"

Mrs Henderson looked relieved. "Oh my dear, I'm so glad you asked. Of course, I couldn't have imposed on you, but the whole thing falls on my shoulders, and there's an absolute mass of work involved."

"Well, I'd be delighted to do anything I can," Emma said. "You needn't have been afraid to ask – I'd like to think I was a full member of the household."

No sooner had Mrs Henderson educated Emma fully in

the plans for the birthday party, than she had to tell her that, after all, Mr Akroyd would not be present.

"It's the greatest nuisance, but he has to go away on business."

"Oh, really?" Emma was surprised.

"He's going to China of all places! Apparently the Chinese government is about to award a contract for a huge bridge somewhere up-country, and it's so important Mr Akroyd feels he must go himself. It could be worth a great deal of money, you see. And for the same reason, he can't put the trip off. If someone's ready to commission work on that scale, you can't keep them waiting on your convenience – especially not the Chinese, I understand. They're very touchy. If he offends the wrong person, the contract could be lost, not only to Akroyd Engineering, but to Britain."

"But couldn't Zara's party be postponed?"

"It could," said Mrs Henderson with an equivocal face, "but Zara won't hear of it. She says it doesn't matter if her father is there or not. Between you and me," she lowered her voice, "I think she thinks there will be a more relaxed atmosphere without him. I wouldn't be surprised if she weren't thinking of inviting some people she knows he wouldn't like."

Since Mrs Henderson was in a confiding mood, Emma dared to go a little further. "I'm surprised that Mr Akroyd is willing to let the party go on without him. Won't it seem rather odd, it being her coming-of-age?"

Mrs Henderson shrugged. "Frankly, my dear, I think he's in such a tizzy about this China business that he hasn't time to worry about a birthday party – even an eighteenth. And of course, she will be 'brought out' in London later in the year, so I suppose he thinks that will be the important date. But it does put more responsibility on the rest of us – especially Gavin. If anything goes wrong, it'll be him that takes the blame."

Emma could not think what might go wrong that Gavin

93

would be blamed for. What did they have servants for? Surely if anyone spilled wine on the carpet or made a glass-ring on an antique commode, Mr Akroyd wouldn't bend Gavin over a chair and give him six of the best for it?

Poppy was excited about the party, and chatted animatedly about the arrangements whenever Emma let her. "I'm not being let to go to the ball," she said, "but I don't care. Zara's friends are really boring, and dancing's stupid. But I'm having a new dress anyway, and Mrs Grainger's making the cake and she said she'd let me help her decorate it."

"Well, that should be interesting."

"Yes. But when I'm eighteen, I'm not going to have a dancing sort of party. I'm going to make everyone come on horseback and have a 'normous gymkhana in the park, and a picnic, and a barbecue with hamburgers and everything, and races and games. And my birthday cake will be all chocolate!"

"Isn't it wonderful to hear her talk about food so enthusi-astically?" Mrs Henderson said, when Poppy repeated all this in her presence. "You've done her so much good," she added to Emma, fondly.

Preparations for the party took Emma away from the schoolroom a good deal in the following weeks – Lady Susan not only gave her blessing to the use of Miss Ruskin as a spare secretary, but did not hesitate to use her herself. Emma was frequently sent on errands for her ladyship, driving into Bury or Cambridge in the Mini to collect things, while her ladyship looked after Poppy. Generally when Emma returned she would find that Lady Susan had wandered off on business of her own, and Poppy would be discovered in the kitchen, kneeling on a stool and messing about with pastry or measuring ingredients for Mrs Grainger. Emma wondered if the child's mother knew where she inevitably ended up, but thought her ladyship would probably sooner even have her child tainted by servants than be inconvenienced herself.

Mr Akroyd departed for Beijing, whence he would travel into the interior in a group made up not only of technicians from his company, but representatives of the Board of Trade, the Foreign Office and a leading High Street Bank. Emma couldn't help wondering whether there would be any danger involved – China was not yet a completely civilised place. Lady Susan wondered anxiously whether he would have time to shop for her in Hong Kong on his way back. Zara wondered urgently whether he would give her her birthday present before he left – which in fact he did. It was a car of her own, a Peugeot 206 with all the gadgets, which Zara received with shrill delight: she actually flung her arms round her father's neck and kissed him, so excited was she. Emma noticed, however, that Gavin did not look pleased, and wondered why. She would not have expected him to be so petty as to begrudge his sister a car.

On the day of the party there were no lessons for Poppy. Emma was up early and put herself at Mrs Henderson's disposal, and it was while they were checking lists together that Mrs Henderson revealed that Emma was expected to attend the party.

"Oh, I couldn't. I didn't expect . . . really, I'd much rather not," Emma stammered in confusion.

Mrs Henderson raised one perfectly groomed eyebrow. "But my dear, you said you wanted to be a full member of the household. I should have thought you'd want to be there."

"Oh—" Emma was embarrassed. "It really isn't my sort of thing. I mean, I'm not one of the family, just a member of staff. I really don't think—"

"Well, I shall be there. And you've worked as hard as I have to make it a success. I really think you will have to put in an appearance. It will be expected."

"But I haven't anything to wear!"

Mrs Henderson laughed. "That's more like it! I thought you really didn't want to go, and I should hate to think we'd knocked all the fun out of you already! Of course, it will be long evening dresses for the ball, but I expect a cocktail frock would do."

"I haven't got either," Emma said.

"Oh dear!" Mrs Henderson seemed really put out. "I wish I'd thought to mention it to you before. I just naturally assumed . . ."

"Look, it really doesn't matter," Emma said firmly. "I would feel very awkward about joining in with the dancing and so on anyway. I'll just pop down at some point and wish Zara a happy birthday, and then disappear. No one will notice."

Mrs Henderson still looked unhappy. "I hate to think of you missing all the fun, especially when you've done so much of the work."

"I really don't mind. Honestly, please don't worry," Emma said as persuasively as she could. The thought of Zara sneering at her, and of Zara's glamorous, predatory girlfriends clustering round Gavin, was not tempting. And an evening spent watching Gavin dance with a succession of gorgeous county females and – worse – enjoying it was not high on her list of fun things to do. She might mean nothing to him, but she didn't have to have her nose rubbed in it.

Zara, looking extremely elegant and, unexpectedly, just a little nervous, stood in the hall welcoming her guests. She was wearing a long dress of yellow silk, and the double strand of pearls which had been her mother's gift to her, and her hair was done up in an elaborate swirl which had taken the hairdresser a couple of hours that afternoon to achieve.

Lights blazed everywhere, and huge flower arrangements lent colour to usually dark corners; stewards and maids buzzed round discreetly, carrying trays of champagne and directing ladies to the cloakroom; the orchestra was playing quietly to itself in the room that would later be full of young people dancing.

Gavin was very much in evidence, filling in the gaps in

Zara's attention span, helping his mother to greet the older guests, making the County feel welcome. The County was arriving in huge Rollers and Bentleys, and was swathed in furs and glittering with diamonds; the younger set zoomed up in BMWs and Range Rovers. Gavin chatted charmingly with them all, young and old, but Emma noticed that he frequently looked about him with a faintly lost air, as though he were expecting someone in particular who hadn't arrived. One of Zara's smart set, Emma supposed, as she watched with Poppy from their hiding place on the first floor landing. Gavin, she thought, looked exceptionally handsome in dinner jacket and black tie: he seemed moulded into it, whereas some of the young men arriving looked as though it was wearing them rather than vice versa. She watched him bow over the hand of a plump pink female in a regrettably short skirt, and his smile did terrible things to her pulse. But his very elegance and beauty eased her in an odd way, because it convinced her, if she needed convincing, that he was way, way out of her league, and that there was nothing for her but to admire him from a distance.

Poppy wriggled with excitement, and whispered to Emma the names and principal habits of those guests she knew, sometimes leaning out so far for a better look that Emma kept a hand on her belt in case she had to grab her. Emma responded with a "Really?" and "Does she?" which was all Poppy seemed to need – fortunately, since Emma's attention was all taken up with watching Gavin and waiting for the guest he seemed to be expecting. At last her vigilance was rewarded. A female arrived whom he greeted with every sign of particularity. It was not one of the Nats and Vics of Zara's set, but an older woman, a tall, dark-haired beauty in a sheath-like dress of turquoise silk.

Emma sighed with sheer admiration, which was almost without a pang. She was glad that it was someone so superior, someone with whom she could not have hoped to compete. She wouldn't have liked Gavin to throw himself

97

away. The dark girl was slim as a withy, very beautiful, elegant, sparkling at throat and wrist with diamonds, and with a lovely smile, to which Gavin responded with tender warmth. He took both her hands with an ease and an eagerness that proved he had known her long, and loved her well, and led her straight away into the the room where the band was playing.

"Who was that girl?" Emma asked, turning to Poppy.

"Which one?" Poppy asked.

"The dark-haired lady that your brother just led away."

"Oh, did he? I wasn't looking." She craned through the banisters. "No. I can't see him. I s'pose it was one of Zara's friends."

"She looked a bit older than Zara."

"Oh well, I don't know then." Poppy was evidently not much interested. She had more important things on her mind. "Emma, can we go down and get something to eat now? I'm abs'lutely *dying* of hunger, and everyone must be here by now. We could sneak down without anybody seeing us."

"I'm afraid not," Emma said. "Not now. It's time you were in bed, and I have to go down and say happy birthday to Zara."

"Oh blow!" Poppy said crossly. "Do you have to? Honestly, she won't care if you do or not."

"I'm sure she won't, but it's the polite thing and I have to do it. But if you're still awake when I come back up, I'll bring you up something from the buffet."

"Oh, brill! What will you bring?"

"I don't know – whatever I can carry most easily, I suppose."

"Sausage rolls," Poppy pleaded. "And cake – chocolate cake."

"I'll see what I can do," Emma promised.

Fifteen minutes later Emma came down the stairs again, feeling like a fish out of water, and hoping not to attract attention. The 'receiving' stage was over, Zara was no longer in the hall, and Lady Susan had retired into the drawing-room with the friends of her generation. But there were still plenty of people standing about the hall, talking, sipping champagne, smoking, laughing at each other's jokes. Emma slipped between them, and was glad to note that they paid her no attention, any more than they noticed the waitresses who drifted about supplying them with full glasses. In her short dress, Emma supposed, she must look like a member of staff – which of course she was – and therefore not to be spoken to.

In search of Zara she went into the dancing-room, and was rewarded – or punished – by the sight of Gavin dancing with the dark-haired girl. He was holding her closely, and they revolved in perfect harmony, not even speaking, his cheek resting against the dark, sleek hair. Despite herself, Emma felt a lump in her throat; and as his head began to turn towards her, she backed hastily out, and went across the hall to another room where there was the sound of bright laughter and talk. There she found Zara in the middle of a group of young men and girls, all shrieking at once and having a whale of a time.

Emma would not have disturbed her, but as she happened to catch Zara's eye and the latter raised an enquiring eyebrow, she decided she'd better get it over with and walked across.

"I just came to wish you a happy birthday," Emma said, "and to hope that you have a wonderful evening. Everything seems to be going OK, doesn't it?"

"Oh yes, thanks," Zara said, looking her up and down. The friends all turned away to give them privacy, apart from the bosom pals Natalie and Victoria, who simply stared as though they couldn't believe their eyes.

"Good," Emma said, trying to shove some warmth into her smile. "Well, I only popped down just to say happy birthday, so I won't keep you any more."

"Oh, but *surely* you're going to stay and have a dance?" Natalie said with heavy irony.

"Oh yes," Victoria added, "I'm sure Zara can find you *someone* to dance with." And she whispered something to Natalie – the name of some poor nerd they despised, Emma supposed – and they both sniggered and clutched each other, thrilled by their own humour.

The only thing was to respond with dignity, Emma thought. "No, I can't stay – I'm not dressed for a formal party," she said. "I'm going back upstairs now."

Zara threw her friends a look, and then grabbed Emma's wrist, turning her away so that Nat and Vic shouldn't hear her words. "Yes," she said in a low voice, "and see you *do* go upstairs. No hanging around Gavin looking like a sick spaniel, because he's just about polite enough to feel he has to ask you to dance. I don't want him bothered by you, d'you understand?"

Only too well, Emma thought. You've got him marked down for one of your giggling friends. Well, I think I can spoil your evening for you. "You needn't worry, Gavin wouldn't ask me to dance. He's very well occupied, dancing with a very lovely girl, and I'm sure he doesn't know anyone else exists."

Zara frowned, and Emma had her moment of triumph. "What girl?" Zara asked crossly.

"Tall, dark and slim, in turquoise silk. They make a lovely couple."

"Oh but that's—" Zara stopped abruptly, and then a canny look stole across her face. "No, you're right, he's sure to be very wrapped up in *that* partner," she said, and turned abruptly away, leaving Emma to pick her way back to the door, glad to have got an unpleasant duty over with. Behind her she heard a burst of shrill laughter, which she had no doubt was Zara and her bosom buddies indulging their fabulous wit again at her expense. As if she cared!

Busy showing she didn't care, Emma did not look where

100

she was going, and bursting out through the door into the hall she ran full tilt into a dress-shirt and had to be held up against the force of the collision. Warm, strong hands gripped her upper arms.

"Steady! Where are you rushing off to?"

Emma's gaze travelled up from the neat, pleated shirtfront to the face that was rarely out of her thoughts these days, and found him smiling, his eyes very bright — left-overs, no doubt, from turquoise-and-diamonds, she thought viciously.

"I wasn't rushing, I was just going back upstairs," she said, trying to sound neutral. She wasn't sure she had succeeded. Gavin set her carefully back on balance, but he did not remove his hands from her arms. She was torn between not wanting him to, and worrying about what the effect on her might be if he didn't.

"Going upstairs? What for?"

"What d'you mean, what for?" she said, annoyed that he was being stupid about it. It must be obvious. "I'm not part of the party. I only came down to say happy birthday to Zara, and now I'm going back up."

"But you mustn't," he said. "I haven't had a dance with you yet, and I've been promising myself that for days. I *wondered* where you were. I kept looking for you. I thought you must be off dancing with some other lucky blighter."

He'd been *looking* for her? He'd been looking for *her*? Emma stared up at him in astonishment. Could he really mean it? But no, she told herself, don't be so simple. You saw how he seized on the turquoise girl the moment he saw her. He's just making a fool of you, being sarcastic.

"I haven't come to the party to dance," she said. She wished he would let her go — it made it hard to think. "You can see I'm not dressed for it."

"Why not?" he argued.

"Oh come," she said shortly, "you can see I'm in a short dress and everyone else is in evening clothes. There's such a thing as being too gallant, you know."

101

He laughed. "Ah, now I feel more at home! I don't feel quite right without Miss Ruskin telling me off about something." She blushed with a complex mixture of vexations, and he said, "Look, please dance with me. I promise no one will notice what you've got on. Honestly, they're all too preoccupied with how they look themselves."

Doubt overcame her. He really seemed to mean it. He really wanted to dance with her. She could no longer feel he meant to make a fool of her; there still remained the likelihood that he was just being polite. She went straight to the bottom line, and said, "But your sister doesn't want me to dance, and it's her party."

"That's the worst excuse you've given me so far." He ran his fingers down her arm and took hold of her hand. "I don't care a fig what Zara thinks, and I don't believe you do, either. Come, please, come and dance."

He led her across the hall to the dancing-room. The band was playing a slow tune. "Good," he said. "I hate that jiggling on the spot stuff. It's no fun unless you can get your arms round your partner." And he drew her to him and stepped away with her to the music, holding her close. Emma tried very hard to tell herself that it meant nothing; but just for that moment, she didn't care. She was going to have this, and enjoy it, and to hell with what came after. She let herself relax into him, feeling the warmth and strength of his body, breathing in the scent of him. How long was a dance tune? Five minutes? Six? Well, if that was all she would ever have, she'd make sure she enjoyed every second of it. He drew her just a little closer, squeezing her hand, not seeming to want to talk, for which she was grateful. They stepped slowly, swaying in sweet harmony, as if they had been dancing together all their lives. Emma closed her eyes in bliss, and time very kindly ceased for a little while to exist.

The dance was over. Sanity flooded back painfully into her

blissed-out brain as the couples around them broke up into chattering groups and began to jostle their way off the floor. She was a member of the household staff, dressed in an unsuitably short dress, and batting right out of her league. She ought to get herself out of Gavin's hair before her glass slippers turned back into clogs and tripped her up.

"Well, thank you for the dance," she said abruptly. "It was very kind of you."

Gavin, who had been smiling, suddenly looked taken aback, and she realised that in her effort to sound matter-of-fact she had in fact sounded cold and sarcastic, as if she *hadn't* enjoyed the dance and *didn't* think it was kind of him.

"I didn't ask you to be kind," he said.

"Well, it was kind, especially as I wasn't dressed properly," she said, "so thank you anyway." It sounded belligerent.

He drew back from her. "It's I who should thank you," he said politely.

Now she had offended him, she thought. Worse and worse! All the warmth had evaporated, and they were suddenly like strangers, trapped by politeness and longing to be elsewhere. How could she be so awkward? She'd better make her escape before she accidentally knocked him down.

"I must go," she said hastily, pulling her hand away from his.

"Oh, not yet, surely?" he said. "Stay and have another dance. No one will mind about your dress. Zara's not even in the room."

"No, I have to go upstairs. I – I promised to look in on Poppy."

"Yes, I see," he said. "Well, I don't want to hold you up, as you're in such a hurry." And he gave an awkward little bow, and turned away.

Emma watched him go. His gait seemed a little offended; but it was better that way. Another dance with him and

103

she might have started to believe her senses instead of her common sense. Arguing herself into a more stable frame of mind, she wriggled away through the crowds and made her way to the buffet. There were already people around it, but she managed to sneak in at one end and, with a nod of complicity at the nearest waiter, who recognised her, she took a plate and loaded it with whatever delicacies were nearest at hand. Then she made her way upstairs, wondering why she could not behave like a normal human being around Gavin Akroyd. She was like a school kid, alternately blushing and surly. The poor bloke had danced with her out of kindness – hadn't he? – and she had snapped at him as if he had insulted her. Oh well, she thought philosophically as she turned the stair, it didn't matter. She was an employee in the house, he didn't have to like her. He'd just think her a bit mad – if he ever thought of her at all, which was unlikely.

As she passed her own room first, she thought she'd stop in and get into her nightdress and dressing-gown before looking in on Poppy. That would prevent her from having any pathetic thoughts of going downstairs again – not even as far as the first landing for a sneaky look at Gavin over the banisters! Quickly she undressed and put on her nightie and the 'sensible' dressing-gown she had bought in case of night emergencies – a full-length, high-necked, woollen thing with big pockets – and taking up the plate of goodies again she went out into the passage and along towards Poppy's room.

The sounds of the party were very faint and far away, for this was the opposite side of the house from the main reception rooms. A good thing, too, she thought, or Poppy would never get to sleep. As she went into the day-nursery, through which she had to pass to get to the night-nursery where Poppy slept, she saw a band of light in the further room, showing at the bottom of the closed door. The floorboards creaked under her feet and the light was quickly doused. Poppy reading in bed, she thought. But she didn't need to be so guilty about it: Emma had said she'd come up and see her.

Quietly she opened the night-nursery door, expecting to see Poppy curled up in bed pretending hard to be asleep. Instead, in the dark room – for it was a moonless night – she could just make out that the bed was empty.

"Hello? Where are you?" she said. The child must be hiding, for a game. "Come on out, I've got the food for you. Lots of goodies!"

She stepped one pace forward into the room, and, just as all the hair rose on the back of her neck with the realisation that there was someone behind her, there was a soft rush of movement and someone grabbed her. Hard hands, adult hands, bruised her, meaning business, and before she could scream something soft was clamped over her mouth. She struggled wildly, thrashing to and fro; the plate of food flew from her hand; she dragged her arm free to grab at the wrist in front of her, trying to tear it from her face, for she was suffocating.

A vile, sickly smell was in her mouth and nose, clinging, cloying, choking. The pad which was pressed over the lower part of her face was impregnated with the stuff. She felt faint, dizzy, she wanted to vomit; she jerked her head against the restraining hands, but she was aware that her struggles were weakening, that she was slipping away from herself. A feeling of nausea and deep despair washed over her, a desperate, desolate sense of being lost; and then a black hole seemed to open under her feet and she fell into it, and down, down into oblivion.

Chapter Nine

Emma drifted back to consciousness slowly and reluctantly. Something had happened, and she didn't want to know what. She floated just under the surface of waking, gradually becoming aware of pain: a raw burning around her mouth and nose; a bitter, biting pain in her wrists and ankles; cramped, bruised soreness from every part of her body that touched the hard, ridged surface she was lying on.

The pain focused her mind, and at once the fear came in, like a radio being switched on. *Danger, danger, danger!* She opened her eyes, but it was pitch dark. As her senses sharpened, she realised that there were voices nearby: two people talking in low, urgent voices. She could hear them strangely muffled, through a heavy, growling noise that transmitted itself through her aching flesh and bones.

"You said it was gonna be all right," someone was complaining. "You said nobody'd hear us. You said everyone'd be on the other side of the house."

"Oh, shut your face! We got the kid, didn't we?"

"Well, I don't like it. What about *her*?"

"She must be the kid's nurse or something. She'll come in useful."

"But suppose they come looking for her?"

"Why should they? She's in her nightie, isn't she? They won't start looking till they don't show up for breakfast. We got hours yet. Now shut up and gimme a fag."

The voices stopped. Now she understood her situation. The growling noise was a motor engine. She was in the back of a van of some sort, lying on the bare floor, her wrists and ankles tied, and some kind of cloth over her head. She had been kidnapped, along with Poppy. Presumably Poppy was also in the back of the van, somewhere near, probably tied up too. Oh God, what would they do to her? What did they want? Money, presumably. Mr Akroyd was rich. If it was money, they would take good care of Poppy, wouldn't they? They wouldn't hurt her. Oh, she prayed not. She hoped it was money. Mr Akroyd would pay to get Poppy back. But what of her own case? Suppose the criminals decided she was expendable? What might they do then? Her stomach curdled in fear.

The van picked up speed, and every time it went over a bump some part of her hit the ridged metal floor. There seemed to be an awful lot of bumps. It was agony; but at least the pain kept her mind off her fear. Then suddenly the front left corner of the van dipped, and the floor heaved up under her. She heard one of the men say, "Look out!" and at the same moment her trussed body was flung sideways, her head struck something hard and sharp, and she slithered sickeningly into unconsciousness again.

Gavin decided to give Emma five minutes, and then go up after her. He blamed himself for the misunderstandings between them. OK, she was very touchy, but after all, as an employee her position was not as straightforward as his. It was up to him to make the situation clear. He was sure she was attracted to him, but she obviously couldn't afford to assume anything, and in his wretched shyness he had failed to make it plain to her that he was interested in her. He must tell her so in words of one syllable, and take it from there.

It was difficult for him to get away from the party, for every few steps he was waylaid by another guest, and he couldn't just brush them aside rudely; but he worked his way as quickly as he could across the hall, and once he got to the foot of the stairs he was home free. He hurried up to the nursery floor. Emma had her own room there, just along the passage from the schoolroom and night-nursery. Her door was shut but the light was on, so at least she had not gone to bed and to sleep already. He knocked; waited; knocked again. He called out, close to the door, "Emma, it's me, Gavin. Can I talk to you?" But there was no reply.

Then he remembered she had said she'd promised to look in on Poppy. Maybe she was there still. He went along the passage, through the day-nursery, and opened the door to the night-nursery. A single glance showed him the bed was empty. He snapped on the light, and in one second had taken in the state of the room: the bedclothes flung back and dragged half off the bed; the framed photograph of Misty on the bedside locker knocked over; the bedside rug rucked into a heap as though by dragging feet; and on the floor in front of him a plate broken into three pieces and various bits of party food scattered about, some of them trodden into the carpet.

The truth scalded into his brain. He turned and ran back to Emma's room, flung the door open, saw that the room was empty and undisturbed, and ran for the nearest telephone. Having summoned the police, he went back down to the first floor landing, almost to the same spot where Emma and Poppy had hidden earlier in the evening, looking for a servant. Better still, he saw Mrs Henderson come out of the room below him, and leaning over the banisters he called urgently, "Jean! Up here!"

She looked up, and saw from his face that something was wrong; so that when he beckoned she obeyed instantly and without fuss, making her way through the guests and quickly up the stairs to him.

"What is it?" she asked. Quickly he told her what had happened. She frowned. "But why d'you think they've been kidnapped? They may have slipped out on some little expedition of their own."

"Emma wouldn't take Poppy out at this time of night. And you can see from the room there's been a struggle. No, I tell you they've been snatched!"

"Shouldn't we at least search a bit before we call the police?"

"I've already called them. If they've been taken, every second counts — you must see that."

She capitulated. "Yes, of course. What do you want me to do?"

Gavin looked relieved. "I don't want the guests to know until they have to, but they mustn't leave the house. Can you quietly round up the servants and post one on each door? And put someone reliable on the front stairs, to stop anyone coming up to the nursery floor. I'm going back up to keep guard, to make sure nothing's touched."

"Yes, all right. What about the police?"

"I've told them to come to the back hall, and no sirens. When they arrive, can you bring them quietly up the back stairs?"

She nodded and went away, and blessing her quiet efficiency, Gavin went back up to the nursery, where he stood at the door, contemplating the real reason why he was sure it was a kidnap. A piece of cake which Emma had brought up to Poppy had been squashed into the carpet, presumably during the struggle, and it bore quite clearly the ridged imprint of a large, man's boot.

When Emma regained consciousness, the van was bumping less violently. They must be on a smoother, better road. She had been thrown or rolled against the side of the van, and now she found that by bracing herself against it and pressing with her heels on the floor, she could steady herself a little, enough to stop herself rolling back and forth. It was very tiring, though, and she couldn't keep it up continuously. Her hands and feet were going dead from lack of circulation, and her head was throbbing abominably. She wanted to drift off

109

to sleep again, and struggled with herself to stay awake and alert. Something might happen; she couldn't just give up.

They were cruising steadily and, from the engine noise, fast. Then she heard one of the men say, "Oh shit! Oh no, oh shit, shit!"

"What?"

"Fuzz, coming up behind us."

"Don't panic. They can't be onto us already."

"What'll we do! What'll we do!" The van lurched under sudden acceleration, and Emma groaned weakly as her head hit the floor again.

"Christ, slow down, you maniac!" the older man said. "D'you want to draw attention to us? I tell you they can't be after us yet. Just drive normally."

"I can lose 'em," the other one pleaded. "Lemme lose 'em!"

"In this thing? Calm down, I tell you! We'll bluff it out."

Emma's heart had risen at this exchange. The police were after them already! She must concentrate, keep conscious. When they were stopped, she'd make such a noise the police would have to hear. They'd be rescued! Oh thank God, thank God!

After a tense silence, the younger voice rose in elation. "They went straight past! They weren't after us!"

"I told you so, you dummy!"

"Thank Christ for that. I thought we'd had it."

"I told you it'd be all right. You panic too easily. All the same, they've seen us now. We'll have to dump this thing."

"But you said—"

"Sooner or later they're going to put out an alert on the van, stupid, and then those coppers'll remember where they saw us." A pause, then the older man went on, "There's a place up ahead. I'll tell you where. We can dump it and you can go out and nick something."

"Aw, Boss—!"

"Stop whining. We'll be OK. Just take it easy. Put the radio on."

Emma's heart sank again. She was so desperately disappointed, her eyes filled with helpless tears, which she struggled against. It was hard enough to breathe, without being choked up with tears. The men went on talking in low voices, but she could no longer hear what they said over the noise of pop music.

Now the motion of the van changed again. She felt it slow, then a hard turn to the left, and then a slow but agonising progress over bumps and hollows. She guessed they had turned off the main road onto a track of some sort. The floor of the van bucked under her like a horse, and she could not brace herself enough to avoid being thrown about. She gritted her teeth, and wondered how Poppy was faring. She had made no sound yet. Was she still unconscious?

At last the van stopped, the engine was cut, and there was blissful stillness. Emma drifted into unconsciousness for a few minutes – she couldn't help it – and when she came to again, it was quite silent. The men must have got out. She wondered if she could do anything to improve the situation – get this cloth off her head, at least – then she could breathe more easily, and see where Poppy was, and whether she was all right. The cloth was a bag of some sort, she thought. If she rubbed it against the floor of the van she might be able to drag it off. The problem was that her head hurt so much, and any movement made the throbbing worse. But she had to try. Slowly, painfully, she worked at it; and as she rubbed and rubbed, she thought about the kidnappers. Two of them, one older and well-spoken, though his accent slipped a bit now and then; the younger one with an ordinary London accent, who sounded a bit stupid – probably he was the strong-arm man. It was he who had been driving, certainly. Was that all, or were they part of a larger gang? And what was going to happen now?

111

The bag came off at last, and Emma drew in a few gasps of fresher, colder air. But that was the only reward for her hard work and pain. It was still pitch dark; she couldn't see a thing. And she was still helpless. She began to cry softly from weariness and fear.

"Now we're getting somewhere," Superintendent Moss said, putting down the phone. "The caterers say one of their vans is missing from the depot. Now if your man at the gate is reliable—"

"He is," Gavin said.

"I'll take your word for it. *He* says nothing came out but catering vans, and all the other vans are accounted for, so it's got to be the one."

"And where does that get us?" Gavin asked. Continuous anxiety was making him weary, slowing his thought processes.

"Well, sir, we've got the van's number now, you see. We can put that out over the radio, so every patrol car will be on the look-out; and thanks to your prompt action we've got the road blocks in place. They won't have got far."

Gavin nodded, but found no comfort in the words. He tried to keep his mind on what had to be done, and what could be done, like fending off enquiries from friends and guests and trying to get hold of his father; but it would keep straying to horrible contemplation of what the villains might do to Poppy and to Emma.

Emma heard the sound of a car engine approaching. For a wild and wonderful instant she thought perhaps it was the police. But it slowed and stopped, and then went whiningly into reverse, then forward again; her imagination supplied the picture of it performing a three-point turn in the track. Then a car door opened and slammed; and then the van doors were abruptly and noisily flung open. There was a breath of fresh, cold air, and light – not much of

112

it, only starlight, but enough, after the pitch blackness, to see by.

A middle-aged man stood there, with a battered-looking face, gold-rimmed glasses, close-cropped grey hair, a dark overcoat.

"All right, let's get 'em out. You take the woman, I'll take the kid."

Behind him the younger man appeared: tall, heavily-built, wearing jeans and an old, padded anorak. He bent towards Emma, and stopped, peering into her face. "She's awake," he said.

"She's got the hood off," the older man said in a tone of menace. "You are a total—" He added an obscenity, which sounded odd in his cultured accent.

"I put it on all right, Boss," the other protested whiningly.

"Yeah, yeah! Well, it's too late now. You'd better gag her, though."

The younger man dragged a handkerchief out of his pocket. Emma eyed it with horror and despair.

"Please," she croaked. "Please don't." The younger man paused, looking at the Boss questioningly. "Please," Emma said again. "Let me breathe. I promise I won't shout."

The Boss looked at her for a moment consideringly, and then he nodded. "All right," he said. Emma saw no compassion in his face; she thought he probably judged she couldn't have shouted if she wanted to.

The younger man climbed up into the van and disappeared behind Emma's line of sight, to reappear a moment later carrying Poppy. She was hooded with what looked like a sugar sack and her arms and legs were tied. The younger man handed her down into the Boss's arms; she made no sound, and was ominously limp.

"What have you done to her?" Emma cried, her voice cracking weakly. The younger man looked down at her with what might have been a faint thread of pity.

"Doped," he said briefly. "She's OK."

"Andy, shut your mouth," the Boss snapped, and walked off with his burden.

"All right, babe, your turn," Andy said. He bent over Emma, pushed his hand under her body, and used the rope around her wrists to jerk her up into a sitting position. She moaned as the rope cut into her already damaged flesh. Still holding her up, Andy climbed out of the van and dragged her towards him until she was on the edge. Then he pulled her round to face him, put his shoulder to her midriff and swung her up. He was very strong, and seemed to make nothing of her weight.

Dangling there, face down over his shoulder, helpless, all Emma could see was the grass over which he was walking. She could smell his sweat, and the tobacco smoke which impregnated his clothes. She tried to turn her head a little, saw thin, scrubby pine trees and gorse bushes. Then she saw the car, a blue saloon, a Rover, she thought. It came closer. The back door was opened. Poppy was lying curled on the back seat, unmoving. Then Andy swung her down, sickeningly, and bundled her in onto the floor. She groaned again as he pushed her legs in, and he muttered, "Shut it! It won't be long." Another little thread of sympathy? But then he threw a blanket over her, and she was alone in the stifling dark again.

She remembered little of the rest of the journey. Cramped, in pain, and starved of oxygen, she was unconscious for much of the time; and when she was conscious, she was hardly aware of where she was or what was happening. At last the car stopped, the engine was cut, and into the stillness there came the sound of birdsong, the massed trilling of the dawn chorus. The door of the car opened, the blanket was drawn away, and light flooded in. Someone was whistling cheerfully. The sound cut through her headache like an ice pick. It was Andy. He reached in and lifted Poppy out, and presumably handed her to his companion; then he stooped

114

over Emma and cut the rope round her ankles and said, "All right, babe, you can walk the rest."

He manhandled her out and tried to put her on her feet, but her legs would not hold her and buckled under her. The world swung dizzily about her; the pressure in her head was agonising and she felt sick. Now the blood was beginning to return to her feet, and the pins-and-needles and the burning pain in her ankles made her moan again, feebly.

"Here, Boss," Andy said, gripping Emma under the armpits, "this one looks a bit rough. And there's blood on her face."

"Hit her head on something, I expect," the Boss said, his voice suddenly close, but without pity.

"Shouldn't we call a doctor or something?"

"Jesus! I wonder how you manage for brains," the Boss sighed in exasperation. "Call a doctor! What did I do to get lumbered with a dickhead like you? Will you hurry up and get her indoors, before the neighbours come round?"

Andy heaved her up roughly, taking it out on her, perhaps, for his telling-off. "Walk, you cow," he snapped, shaking her. She stumbled forward, most of her weight taken by him, her feet flopping and dragging stupidly as she tried to control them. Through a daze of pain and dizziness she caught a glimpse of the house, grey stone and creeper, coming towards her. She felt dimly that she ought to be trying to notice things in case it might help, but the darkness was swaying back towards her like a big, soft, welcome cloud.

Only half-conscious, she was dragged into the house, up the stairs, and into a room, where there was a bed pushed up against the wall. Poppy was lying on the bed, unhooded but still tied. Andy threw Emma down on the bed beside her, rolled her onto her side, cut the rope round her wrists, and said, "There you are, babe. You can untie the kid. She's all yours."

Emma was aware of him leaving the room, heard the door close and the click of the lock, but for the life

115

of her she couldn't move, not an inch, not a muscle. She ought to get up and untie Poppy, she knew, but the blackness was swirling back, and she had no strength to resist it.

Chapter Ten

Someone was kicking her, and calling her. It seemed unkind. She didn't want to wake up: she knew that, though she didn't know why. She tried to tell them to leave her alone and go away, but all that came out was a gutteral noise.

"Wake up! Wake up!"

She tried to roll over, away from the nuisance, and pain shifted inside her head like a rock sliding down a slope. "Oh no," she muttered. "No, don't."

"Emma, *please*! Please wake up! Oh, please speak to me!"

It was Poppy's voice. Understanding slowly seeped in. Poppy was nudging her and calling her. But why? Was she late for breakfast? She tried to open her eyes but the light stabbed the inside of her skull and made her cry out. And then she remembered why she so deeply, definitely didn't want to wake up. They had been kidnapped. And, oh my God, Poppy was still tied up! How long had she been sleeping while poor Poppy cried and called to her? She must wake up, she must help her.

She rolled onto her side, tried to get her elbow under her and push herself up. The pain smashed around inside her head as if someone was playing squash with it, and as she opened her eyes a slit, nausea came rushing up like an eager crowd on the first day of the sales.

"It's all right," she muttered thickly. "All right, Poppy. Just wait a minute."

"Oh, Emma, I thought you were dead!" Poppy cried, a

lifting voice of relief with a sob in it. Emma, hanging her head, feeling like death, was able to imagine how frightened the child had been, with her only protector lying like a log beside her. Emma managed to get her eyes open a little further, managed some species of smile, though the throbbing, blinding pain in her head was something that had to be felt to be believed. Poppy's tearstained face was a few inches from hers, her cheek to the pillow, her hands still tied behind her back. "You were so white and still, and I called you and called you, but you wouldn't wake up. I was so frightened!"

The memory of her fear set her sobbing again, though perhaps it was partly relief. Emma managed to reach out a hand and pat the nearest bit of Poppy to her.

"It's all right," she said again. "It's all right now. Just give me a minute, and I'll untie you."

It took a good five minutes before Emma was able to move herself. Then she inched herself round so that she could lean against the wall, and Poppy wriggled round to present her back to her. The knots had pulled tight, of course, and Emma's fingers felt like uncooked sausages – thick and limp, useless for the task. While she worked away at them, slowly and doggedly, Poppy asked her what had happened.

"We've been kidnapped," Emma told her. There seemed no point in sugar-coating it. "Two men came and took us away."

"Where are we?"

"I don't know. They took us in a closed van. I couldn't see anything. And you were drugged."

"I remember now," Poppy said with a dry sob of fright. "I was waiting for you to come up, and I must have fallen asleep, and then suddenly there was somebody there, standing by the bed, and I tried to scream but they put something over my mouth and there was this awful smell—"

"Yes, I know. Chloroform, I think. But that wouldn't keep

you unconscious all that time. They must have injected you with something, I suppose, once you'd stopped struggling."

"It's horrible," Poppy whispered. "Why would anyone want to kidnap us?"

"Well, you for money, I should think. They'll ask your father for a lot of money to get you back."

"Daddy's very rich," she said.

"And they took me because I disturbed them. I came up with your goodies from the buffet and they grabbed me from behind and chloroformed me, too. I woke up in the van, tied up and with a bag over my head."

"Poor Emma," Poppy said.

"Poor Poppy," she replied. "Ah, at last, it's coming. Yes – there. Done!"

Poppy pulled her arms forward, and then at once began to writhe in agony. "Oh, they've gone dead! Oh Emma – oh—!"

Emma did her best for her, rubbing her arms as vigorously as she had strength for. She knew the agony of returning blood, and the horrible feeling of a dead limb flopping about like a landed fish at the end of one's body. "Keep flexing your fingers," she advised. She needed to rest. "Can you rub for yourself now?"

When Poppy was sufficiently recovered to sit up, still rubbing her forearms with her hands, she looked at Emma with wide, grave eyes and said in a small voice, "What's happened to your head?"

"I bumped it in the van," Emma said vaguely. "Why?"

"You've got blood all in your hair."

Emma reached a careful hand towards the centre of pain and found her hair partly sticky, partly wet. She felt queasy, but tried to make light of it for Poppy's sake.

"It probably looks worse than it is," she said, but she swayed dizzily. Poppy's hands came up to her shoulders.

"You lie down. I'll do the other rope myself. I expect I'm better at knots than you anyway. My fingers are smaller."

Emma didn't argue. The exertion had made her sweat. She lowered herself gingerly to the horizontal and closed her eyes. After a bit Poppy said, "Don't worry, I bet someone will rescue us soon. I bet Gavin will come after us. As soon as he knows what's happened, he'll come."

Emma didn't speak. Poppy's faith in her brother was touching, but what likelihood was there that anyone would discover they were missing until morning? And by then the trail would be cold. It would be a matter of waiting until they were ransomed. But Mr Akroyd was in China. Could Gavin authorise the payment? It would depend how much was demanded, she supposed. Otherwise, they would have to wait until Mr Akroyd came back. Did the kidnappers know he was away from home?

It was a fruitless area for conjecture. She turned her mind from it and contemplated her injuries instead. How bad were they? A cut scalp and concussion from the blow on the head. Deep bruises and ragged abrasions on her wrists and ankles from the ropes. Bruises on hips, ribs and elbows from being tossed about in the van. A sore, chapped area around her mouth, like sunburn, from the choloroform. And oh, she was thirsty!

"Wish I had a drink of water," she muttered. Poppy had finished untying her legs and was rubbing the life back into her feet. She looked at Emma, and was frightened. She looked very bad. Suppose she died? No, she mustn't die! But Emma was helpless: it was up to Poppy. She mustn't panic, she must think logically, just as if it was Misty who was hurt, and depending on Poppy to help him. She tried to remember what she knew about first aid. All that blood in Emma's hair looked very bad, but hadn't she read somewhere that head injuries always bleed a lot? And that it was better if it did bleed, rather than blood collect inside? She was sure she'd read that somewhere. She leaned over Emma and gently touched her head. Emma made a small noise, like a grunt.

"It's only me, don't worry. Just let me feel your head," Poppy said. She probed and peered through the matted hair, and found the gash, which looked rather sickening, but seemed more or less to have stopped bleeding. Well, that was a relief, anyway. But perhaps it ought to be bathed. And Emma had wanted a drink of water. "I'm going to make them come and bring us some water," she said aloud. "You just lie still and don't worry." It made her feel much better, much less frightened, to be taking charge like this, taking care of Emma. Emma needed her, so she must be brave.

Emma didn't answer – she seemed to have gone to sleep again. Poppy got off the bed and examined the room. It was quite bare, except for a wooden kitchen chair, and the bed, which was made up with blankets but no sheets, and just the one pillow, covered in striped ticking, but no pillow case. The walls were plain plaster, painted white. The floor was bare boards. There was one window, small, dust-caked, and with bars over it, and in the wall opposite the window was a plain door of unpainted wood with a brown plastic knob. The room was roughly eight feet by six, but an odd shape – the walls weren't parallel.

Poppy went and tried the door without any hope, and it didn't budge at all – in fact the door knob didn't even turn. She knelt and put her eye to the keyhole but could see nothing but blackness. She crossed to the window and pulled the chair under it so she could stand on it, the better to see out. The window was only about twelve by eighteen inches, and was set on the outside of the wall, while the bars were fitted to the inside, so the whole thickness of the wall – about a foot, Poppy thought – was between the bars and the glass. Through the dusty panes she could see the branches of a tree waving gently in the breeze, and the blue sky beyond. They were not on the ground floor, then.

So much for that. There was obviously no way out except by the door. Poppy went to the door and began to bang on it with her fist. After a while her fist started to get sore, so she changed to kicking it and yelling.

It was a long time before she got any response, and she was growing both tired and discouraged. But at last there was a loud thump on the outside of the door, which startled her, and a voice, curiously muffled, said, "Stop that bloody row! Whaddya want?"

"Lots of things," Poppy shouted back boldly. "Food and water and bandages. My friend is sick. Open the door and let me talk to you."

There was a pause, and then the voice said, "Stay back from the door. Go and sit on the bed."

Poppy retired as ordered, and after a moment the door opened a crack, and a tall, heavy young man sidled through, closing it behind him. Poppy saw with a thrill which was not all fear that he was holding a gun, pointed towards her.

"Is that a real gun?" she couldn't help asking. "I bet it's not a real gun."

His eyes narrowed. "Don't get bloody smart with me," he said. "You got a lot of mouth for a kid in big trouble."

"It's not me that's in trouble," Poppy retorted. "It's you that'll get it when they catch you."

"Forget that – they ain't gonna catch us."

"They always do," Poppy said, trying to sound matter-of-fact. "What's your name?"

"Andy." He leaned against the door, and jiggled his gun up and down. "I know yours, Miss Arabella Akroyd. What kind of a name is that?"

"It's as good a name as yours."

"It's a bloody mouthful. Whadda they call you for short? Arry?" He grinned at his own joke.

"You can call me Arry if you like," Poppy said. "Now can we get down to business?"

"Whatever you say," he said, seeming to be enjoying the exchange. "What d'you want?"

"First, some hot water and disinfectant and clean cloths

to clean my friend's head wound. I think it might need stitching."

"It can go on wanting," he said harshly. "Whajjer think this is, a game?"

"You don't want her to die, do you?"

"I couldn't give a stuff. It's not her that's worth a fortune." But he looked sidelong at Emma as she lay, white-faced and unconscious on the bed. "That's a lotta blood," he muttered.

"If she dies, you'll be in worse trouble when they catch you," Poppy urged.

"Stuff all that 'when they catch me' business." He looked uneasy suddenly. "What are you up to? D'you know something?" He looked round the room as though he might find some clue. And then he seemed to reassure himself, and laughed. "Listen, if you think someone's going to come and rescue you, you can forget it. They'll never find us here – and even if they found *us*, they'd never find *you*."

He sounded so sure that Poppy's small courage sank. He saw it, and his grin widened.

"All right, Arry, mate, I'll bring you some grub. And I'll see what I can do about water and rags and stuff. I don't promise, but I'll see what I can do. Now sit down on the bed and don't move."

When he had gone, she jumped up and went to examine the door more closely. She found that one of the knotholes was in fact a spy hole. She put her eye to it but could see nothing – she supposed it only worked one way. But it meant there was no chance of rushing him when he came with the food. She went back to the bed and looked down at Emma, worried. Emma opened her eyes.

"You were brilliant," she murmured. "I don't know how you could be so brave."

"Oh, he wasn't so tough," Poppy said airily. "I'm not scared of him."

"Well, be careful," Emma said, closing her eyes again.

Poppy was one of the television generation, for whom, Emma feared, reality was always one pace distant, a pale shadow of the silver screen. "That's a real gun, you know."

"He won't shoot me," Poppy said confidently. "Not if he wants the money."

Emma felt that, on the whole, it was better for Poppy to keep her spirits up, so she didn't say any more. There were other things that could be done short of shooting, some of which might make shooting seem almost preferable.

"We've found the van," Superintendent Moss said with quiet pride. "Abandoned in some scrub woodland on the edge of Thetford Forest. The locals call it Pratchett's Wood – d'you know it?"

He addressed his remark to Gavin and Mrs Henderson: Lady Susan was keeping to her room in a state of collapse, and Zara was keeping out of everyone's way, though Gavin could not be sure what her feelings about the affair were.

"Yes, I know it," he replied.

"I told you they wouldn't get far," Moss went on. "One of our mobiles went past it shortly before the general alert went out. They remembered it, and went back to check."

"But you said it had been abandoned?" Mrs Henderson queried. "You mean you haven't found Poppy and Emma?"

"No, the van was empty" Moss admitted. "Forensic are going over it now for anything that might help us. But there are tyre tracks of a car there as well, so we're assuming they transferred them into another vehicle at that spot."

"So you've lost them." Gavin's voice was blank with defeat.

"It's not as bad as that. You see, a neighbouring small-holder has reported his car stolen—"

"But—" Gavin began the obvious objection.

The Superintendent put up his hand. "Bear with me. The tracks of the second car showed that the tyres didn't match –

it had three of one design and one of a different pattern. We checked with the smallholder, and his car had three Dunlops and a Michelin. We're checking the tyre patterns, now, but we're pretty sure it was the same car, which means we've got a description and a number."

"When was the car stolen?"

"Ah, that's the interesting bit! The smallholder came in late from the pub, about half past twelve; and owing to the amount of beer he'd sunk, he had a restless night. Got up to go to the bathroom around three o'clock, and glancing out of the window, saw the car had gone. So it gives us a time period during which the car must have been nicked. Also, it proves—"

"That changing to the second car wasn't the original plan," Gavin supplied.

Moss nodded. "You're quick! Yes, otherwise they'd have had one ready."

"But where does it get us?" Mrs Henderson said unhappily. "They've still got away. They could have gone clear to the other end of the country by now."

Moss almost grinned. "I don't think so. The smallholder tells us that the petrol tank was almost empty – he'd meant to fill her up today. He reckons there was only enough to do about ten miles at most. We're checking now to see if they filled up anywhere, but with the two victims in the car I think it's unlikely. And if they didn't, we've got them inside a pretty small radius. We'll throw a net round them and gradually draw it closed. They won't get away, I can promise you that."

"God, I hope not," Gavin said. He felt miserably responsible. With his father away, it had been up to him to keep everyone safe. They had never particularly worried about security. They had guarded against burglary, but kidnapping had never entered anyone's head. He saw now that they should have thought of it, especially on a night like that of Zara's party, when dozens of people, many of them

125

strangers, were coming and going about the house. What would his father say when he got back?

As if picking up on Gavin's thought, Superintendent Moss said, "Have you had any luck in contacting your father yet?"

"We know where he is now, and we've sent a message. We're waiting to get confirmation that it's reached him," Gavin said. "I expect he'll start back as soon as he gets it, but it will take time, a day at least, probably longer. Until then—"

"Yes sir," Moss said soothingly. "I'm quite happy to deal with you."

Gavin met his eyes. "But will the kidnappers be?"

In the afternoon, when Emma had slept a little, Andy returned, but this time with his boss. His demeanour was subdued, and the interview was much less friendly, and Poppy kept close to Emma all through it, evidently beginning to feel something of the danger they were in.

There was nothing humane or approachable in the Boss's face. It was lined with experience, but the experiences were evidently not happy ones. His nose had been broken and set badly at some point, and there was an old scar running up the side of his forehead and into his hair; but the lines from his nose to his mouth corners were harsher than scars, and his eyes behind the glasses were as cold as a snake's.

"Right, girls," he said, swinging the chair one-handed under him and sitting on it backwards, with his arms folded along the back. Andy leaned against the closed door, covering Emma and Poppy with his gun. In the small room Emma could smell Andy's anxious sweat and the Boss's overdone aftershave; but more than that she could feel the menacing presence of the two men so acutely it was like a third and more overpowering smell. It made her shiver. And there was nothing pleasant about the way he called them 'girls'. It was hard and contemptuous: as if he

126

were emphasising the fact that in his position he could call them whatever he damn well liked.

"Right, girls, let's have some straight talking. You know the score, I imagine. We've borrowed the kid for a bit, and we expect her old man to pay a nice little fortune to get her back in one piece. We know who *you* are," he went on, nodding at Emma. "You're the governess and you're a bloody nuisance, but since you've stumbled into this you can make yourself useful by looking after the kid. Right?"

Poppy, pressed against Emma's side, was trembling, but she spoke up now in a mixture of fear and anger. "You won't get away with this! They'll find us soon, and then you'll go to prison!"

"Shut your face!" the Boss snapped. His eyes chilled Emma. "You, you'd better keep her quiet if you know what's good for her. I don't have much patience with lippy kids."

Emma found Poppy's hand and squeezed it warningly. Andy was just stupid and would do what he was told, but this one, she thought, was the real criminal. He would probably enjoy hurting people.

"Better," the Boss said, scanning them stonily. "Now listen. If you give us no trouble, you won't get hurt, understand me? You'll get food, water, whatever you need. And you won't be touched. I want your old man to get you back in the condition we found you. But if either of you try anything, or make trouble, or if *you*—" Poppy shrank from the cold gaze that rested on her, "give me any lip, you'll be sorry you were born. So take your choice."

He seemed to be waiting for an answer, so Emma, pressing Poppy's hand, said quietly, "We won't give you any trouble."

"Sensible girl," the Boss said with a smile that did not warm Emma in the least. "Wise of you to realise that you're expendable. And you'd better get it into the kid's head that, OK, we want to keep her in mint condition, but if she does anything to annoy us, we can still shoot you. Not to kill,

127

necessarily. We can just shoot you where it'll hurt. You get me? She messes up, *you* get it. Savvy?"

Poppy was trembling like a leaf now, and Emma put her arm round her and held her close. "All right," she said with a spurt of anger, "I said we wouldn't give you trouble. Can't you see you're frightening her?"

"Quite the mother lioness protecting her cub, aren't we?" the Boss sneered. Andy grinned, knowing there was a joke without necessarily understanding it. "All right, you can write the note, since you're the woman of action. We want the kid's old man to know we've got you safe and sound."

A writing pad and biro were produced, and under dictation, Emma wrote:

The kidnappers have Arabella and me securely hidden. We have not been harmed, and no harm will come to us if you follow instructions. They are demanding a ransom of a million pounds—

At that point, Emma looked up in surprise. The Boss met her eyes with quick understanding.

"Didn't know he was that rich, eh? Well, when you go back, you can ask him for a raise – if you get out of here in one piece, that is."

The rest of the dictation covered the details of how the money was to be paid. It was, as far as she could tell, a straightforward deal: they seemed only to want the money, and to have no interest in hurting either of them. She hoped it was true, and drew what comfort she could from it; and hoped, also, that the Boss had his facts right about Mr Akroyd's fortune. She signed the note, and then Poppy signed underneath 'Arabella Akroyd'. By unspoken agreement, neither of them had revealed that she was always called Poppy. They didn't quite know why, but it seemed something they should keep to themselves.

When he had examined the note carefully, the Boss tucked it away, gestured to Andy, and they both left. Alone, Emma and Poppy sat in silence for a long time, their arms round

128

each other. Poppy had discovered that things in real life had a particular hardness and reek that television did not portray. Emma was trying to rack her aching brains for something they could do that would help.

They seemed to her particularly helpless because they weren't even dressed. Poppy was in her Rupert Bear pyjamas, Emma in her nightdress and dressing-gown. Fortunately it was warm in the little room, even a little stuffy. They had no possessions of any sort, she thought – until, putting her hand in her dressing-gown pocket for her handkerchief, she found the curved, hard shape of her nail-scissors. She'd forgotten about them. On the morning of the party she'd had her bath, and then put her dressing-gown on and sat by the window while she cut her finger- and toenails. She must have put the scissors into the pocket without thinking, and there they were still.

For no very good reason, the discovery cheered her a little. It was hardly conceivable they could be used as a weapon: the short, curved blades would not put anyone out of action, even if she could get near enough to use them. But somehow, some time, in some way, they might be useful. Emma felt strangely better for this small secret as she returned the scissors to her pocket, and hoped that the men would not think of searching her.

Chapter Eleven

Andy brought them a meal of bread and butter and tea in the evening, and left them without a word, having hardly looked at them. Perhaps the Boss had told him to keep his distance. Certainly they were being careful: the bread and butter was brought in Andy's hand and simply put down on the bed – no plates or knives – and the tea was ready-poured in two big plastic mugs. Nothing that might possible serve for a weapon.

Neither felt hungry, but both were very thirsty, and drank the tea gratefully. Guessing there would be nothing more that night, Emma warned Poppy to sip the tea rather than gulp it – it would be more thirst-quenching that way. When they had drunk, they felt their hunger, and ate the bread; and then, since there didn't seem to be anything else to do, they lay down on the bed. At first Emma tried to keep up a conversation, thinking it might do them good to talk, but she couldn't think of anything but their predicament, and without any input from Poppy the attempt soon failed, and they lay side by side in silence, staring at the ceiling.

From the light outside, Emma guessed it to be about eight o'clock. There was no light in the room, so presumably after sunset they would be left in darkness. She thought that would be unpleasant; then she wondered if any use could be made of the fact. But it all boiled down to the impossibility of jumping the man with a gun. Her eyes roved aimlessly over the ceiling. It was odd for a room to be built without a light; there was no scar in the plaster where a fitment had been taken out, so it must always have been like that. It was an odd room altogether – too small for a bedroom, too big for a cupboard, and such a strange shape, like a bit of a room snipped off at random.

A bit of a room. The idea meandered round her brain. Could it be that the wall with the door in it was a false wall, built across an existing room to cut this part off? But for what purpose? No light, not even an electric wall socket; even in a box-room you would want a light, wouldn't you? OK, it had daylight, but you couldn't guarantee you'd always come looking for your old football boots or photograph albums in daylight.

She got off the bed and went across to examine the wall, tapped it here and there with her knuckles, scratched at it with a fingernail, applied her eye uselessly to the peephole and keyhole. She tried the other walls, examined the window closely, and then stood, staring in thought.

"What is it? What are you doing?" Poppy asked lethargically from the bed.

"Oh, I was wondering about this room. I think perhaps it was purpose-built for us, by putting up this wall across the corner of a bigger room. The plaster's different from the other three walls, and the paint looks new. And that window's obviously very old. Say they had a room with a barred window already in it, and they just made this – this cell by partitioning it off?"

"Why would they do that?"

"Well, to make it secure for one thing. There's nothing in this room, nothing at all, that we could use." Not even a light flex to hang themselves with, she thought, but she didn't say that to Poppy. "And for another – we don't know what it looks like from the outside – out in the other room, I mean."

Poppy sat up, looking interested. "A secret room!"

Emma nodded. "Maybe."

"It must be!" Poppy said. "Andy said even if the police

found *them*, they'd never find *us*. That must be what he meant − that we're hidden in a secret room."

"Poppy, listen," Emma said, turning to her suddenly. "This wall doesn't sound solid to me. I think it's only lath and plaster. I think I could make a hole in it with my nail scissors."

"Big enough for us to get through?" Poppy's voice was an excited whisper.

"No, that would take days with only the nail scissors, and they'd notice it before it got anywhere near big enough, to say nothing of the mess. No, I just meant a small hole, just big enough to see through."

"What good would that do?" Poppy said, disappointed.

Emma looked helpless. "I don't know. At least we'd know what was on the other side. Whether they live in there or in another part of the house. Whether anyone else comes in."

Poppy's expression said she didn't think much of that for a plan, but she said kindly, "Well, if you think it'll help . . ."

"It's a choice between doing that or doing nothing," Emma said. Baldly, that was it.

"Anyway, Gavin's sure to find us soon," Poppy said comfortingly. "Are you going to start now?"

"Yes. I'll do it in the corner and down near the floor, where it won't be so obvious. You put your ear to the door and tell me if you hear anyone coming."

It was harder than she had expected to make any impression with her inadequate tool; and bending down made her head ache again. When it grew dark she gave up the attempt. They got into bed and slept almost at once, for they were more tired than they knew.

Emma slept heavily and dreamlessly, and woke at first light with Gavin's name on her lips. She didn't know at first where she was. She thought she was back in Muswell Hill, and listened for a half-awake moment for the traffic noises. Then she came slowly to the realisation of the truth, and it rolled heavily onto her heart. The flat seemed so far in the past – two lifetimes away, since Long Hempdon was one lifetime. What was happening out there? What were the police doing? Were they on the trail, or were she and Poppy entirely lost? What was Gavin thinking, feeling, doing? Would she ever see him again? She thought back over the time she had known him, and in particular of that last night, when they had danced together. Looking back with the clarity her present situation had brought to her, she knew that he cared for her, and that she had long been falling in love with him. She had wasted the opportunity of Zara's party, thrown Gavin away with both hands because of her – what? Pride? Touchiness, more like: a ridiculous, monumental chip on her shoulder, legacy of being dumped by Chris. If she had danced again with him as he had asked her, and relaxed, and gone with the moment, who knows what might have happened?

That thought gave her pause. If she hadn't run off upstairs in a huff, or whatever she had run off in, she would not have stumbled on the kidnappers. She would not have been here now, but home safe in bed. But Poppy would be here alone, terrified, at the mercy of whatever the kidnappers chose to do to her. Well, to be honest, she was not much safer with Emma there, but at least she was infinitely less frightened. Emma would not have had her face this alone for anything, not even for her own life. Her leaving Gavin as she did had served its purpose.

She squeezed her eyes shut to keep back the tears. He would have come to the same conclusion. And he loved Poppy like a father. He must be frantic with worry, raging with helpless frustration. Had he been lying sleepless, thinking of them – of her? Was that why she had woken saying his name?

If only she could get a message to him; if only she could get a message out of the house, that someone might find and take to him. Could she perhaps break the window and throw something out? But she had no paper, in any case, and no pencil. She had nothing in the world but a handkerchief and a pair of scissors . . .

The idea came to her, and she rejected it at first, but then came back to it with reluctance. She looked at Poppy, and saw that she was still sleeping peacefully, and then got up carefully, so as not to disturb her, and went over to the window where the light was better. She sat down on the chair and took the handkerchief and scissors out of her pocket. She looked at the point of the blades, and at her hands, and finally at the torn and bruised places on her wrists. With a shuddering sigh she picked up the scissors and gritted her teeth.

It was hopeless. After an agonising few minutes she had to admit it was hopeless. Had she had paper, it might have worked, but on the cotton of the handkerchief her blood just spread in blodges and smears. It was impossible to write a legible word. She shook her aching wrist and bit her lip, trying not to cry. She had the ridiculous feeling that Gavin was out there somewhere near at hand, and that if she didn't get a message to him he would walk past and never know she was there.

She looked again at the scissors and the now brown-spotted handkerchief; and after a moment her expression lightened. She dug the point of the blade into the cloth and began to cut carefully. It was difficult, more difficult than she had expected. She had to make the letters large to make them recognisable one from another, and that meant she could not make many of them. But by the time the sun came round into the room she had cut the words HELP POPPY out of the handkerchief. When it was crumpled up nothing was visible, but spread it out on a flat surface and the letters were shaky but legible. She rolled the frayed scraps together and thrust them, with the handkerchief, into her pocket. She still had to think of a way to break the window.

134

Gavin had a restless night, and finally fell asleep at about three o'clock, to be woken, feeling heavily unrested, by the dawn chorus. At once his mind began to churn over the problem all over again. Yesterday had been a full and tiring day; but at least his father was on his way home, and should be arriving this morning. Gavin would be glad to have someone to share the burden. Jean Henderson did all she could, but she was not family, the responsibility could not be hers. Lady Susan was useless, of course. The very thought of intruders in her house threw her into hysteria, and though she was enough of a mother to be worried about Poppy, her anxieties, it transpired, were far more centred on the twins. The one time she had appeared downstairs yesterday had been to beg the Superintendent with tears and a voice almost off the scale to put an armed guard on the boys' school, in case the kidnappers decided one was not enough. Moss had taken it very calmly, and assured her that he had already thought of that, and that a plain-clothes man and a uniformed patrol were even then setting up operations around Jack and Harry. Lady Susan had taken a great deal of reassuring. One minute she had begged Gavin to go and fetch the boys home, the next she had wanted them shipped off to Scotland to her father's shooting estate; and she could hardly be satisfied without an open telephone line to the school with a constant running commentary on the boys' safety.

Yes, it had been an emotionally full day, he thought wearily, turning over in search of a rest that eluded him. Particularly stimulating had been the conversation he had had with Superintendent Moss on the subject of Emma. How much did Gavin know about her? How had she been recruited to the household? Had her references been taken up? Who were her friends? Had she had any visitors since she'd been here, or been seeing anyone regularly? Had she written any letters, made any phone calls, and who to?

"Look here," Gavin had said at last, "I know what you're

suggesting, but it's ludicrous. Emma Ruskin is a good, kind, sensible, honest person. She loves Poppy and Poppy loves her."

Moss regarded him steadily. "I'm glad to have your opinion on that, sir," he said, and Gavin felt riled.

"Look, I know her and you don't!"

"You've known her for – how many weeks? Not quite a month yet, is it?"

"Some people you know in a very short time. I tell you she has nothing to do with this! In any case, they've taken her too, don't forget!"

"Yes, well that would be what you'd expect, if she was involved. Otherwise she might end up with some difficult questions to answer," said Moss reasonably. "You must admit, it's funny that this happens just after she joins your household—"

"Coincidence, that's all."

"Maybe. But we're pretty certain there was an inside connection somewhere. The kidnappers knew the layout of the house, knew that the party would be going on—"

"Good God, half the County knew the party would be going on!"

"Quite. But the timing, the route, the stealing of the catering van, taking them out down the backstairs – it all smells of an inside job to me. And your Miss Ruskin's got all the information needed, she's new, and she's never been a governess before, so you said. Funny a school teacher should suddenly give that up for a live-in job, don't you think?"

"No, I don't think it's funny at all," Gavin said angrily.

Moss nodded sympathetically – or was it pityingly? Got it bad, his expression said. "Well, maybe you're right. But I think we'll have a little look into Miss Emma Ruskin's background anyway, see what we can find out. Ruskin – is that an Irish name?"

"Not as far as I know," Gavin said. "What are you suggesting?"

136

"Kidnappers sometimes want other things than money," Moss said non-committally.

For the rest of the day, the news had only been negative. No reports of the smallholder's missing car being seen. No reports of it filling up anywhere, or of anyone within the radius buying petrol in a can. Nothing of any use discovered by the forensic team from the dumped catering van. No idea of who the kidnappers might be. No contact yet by letter or phone with a ransom demand. It was horribly frustrating.

Gavin abandoned the attempt to go back to sleep, and sat up. He had left his curtains open last night, and the early light streamed in, and the birdsong was fading now to daytime levels. He went to the window and threw it open, and smelled the marvellous freshness of damp earth and grass and clean morning air. Where were they? Were they all right? Would he ever see them again? The sweetness of the morning should have restored him, but all he could think was how Emma was a town girl, and whether he would ever have the chance to teach her to love the countryside.

For the prisoners, the day passed slowly. Nothing broke their solitude but the visits of Andy with food — and dull food it was, nothing hot except mugs of tea. There was bread and butter and slices of Spam for breakfast, bread and butter and corned beef for lunch. Emma asked for some fruit, and got a blank look and a shrug from Andy. If they had to stay here long, Emma thought, they would get spots.

In between they were left alone with their thoughts, their fears, and the tedium. The boredom was hard to bear. There was nothing to do; and Poppy was at the age when children are full of physical energy which needs burning off by running about and romping. Being shut up in this tiny room with no space to stretch her legs was torture to her. Emma did her best to devise ways of passing the time. She did lessons with Poppy from memory; they played 'I Spy' and 'Twenty Questions' and 'Nebuchadnezzar', sang songs

137

and recited what poetry they could remember by heart. But still the hours dragged, and they grew more and more tense, waiting for news, waiting for danger.

For Emma the worst thing in this time of waiting was the lack of toilet facilities. They were not allowed outside the room: Andy brought in a bucket with a lid. It was dreadful to Emma to have to use it there in the room with Poppy gallantly turning her back and humming loudly to give Emma what privacy was possible. It didn't bother Poppy, but Emma was not a country girl, and had no history of 'going behind a hedge'. She found the whole thing distressing and humiliating, and begged their guard to let her go to the WC, offering every safeguard she could think of, but he would not let her out.

Time crawled by. They felt dirty, tired, restless; afraid when they were not bored, always helpless and frustrated. Emma had not thought of a way to break the window. It was too far behind the bars to reach, and the bars were too narrow even for Poppy's arm to go through. She thought of trying to wrench a leg off the chair and break the glass with that, but it was too sturdily made and she hadn't the physical strength. The hole in the wall did not prove a success. All she could see through it was a few feet of floorboards, and she did not dare start another further up for fear it would be noticed. Already she was in dread that Andy would see the first one, for she had no way of concealing it: if she had moved the bed, he would have been bound to want to know why.

Mr Akroyd arrived home mid-morning, grey with exhaustion and worry. He clasped Gavin's hand in a moment of silent sympathy and support.

"This is the devil of a business," he said. Gavin bowed his head.

Lady Susan actually came downstairs to greet her husband, and clung to him, pouring out her fears and griefs.

He bore with it patiently for a time, but then caught Mrs Henderson's eye over her shoulder and gestured to her to take his wife away. Then he went to closet himself with the Superintendent to talk about the ransom demand which had arrived.

"I'm ready to pay," he said at once. "I want that understood. I don't care what it costs, I want my little girl back."

"They're asking for a million," Moss said non-committally.

Akroyd blanched a little, but swallowed and said, "It'll take a bit of getting – I don't keep money idle. But if that's the only way—"

"We'll see," Moss said. "There's no harm in starting your arrangements, but we hope to get them both back without that."

"I don't want any chances taken," Mr Akroyd said sharply.

"I quite understand your feelings, sir. Nobody wants any harm to come to the hostages, but we have a proper method for dealing with these things. You must leave it to us. If the time comes when we think the money should be paid, we'll advise you accordingly, but for the moment we haven't come to the end of our enquiries. If we can get them back, *and* nab the villains, without the money, I take it you'd be even better pleased?"

"That goes without saying." Mr Akroyd mopped his sweating upper lip with a handkerchief. "I worked hard for every penny I own, and I don't fancy giving it away to some layabout who's never done an honest day's work in his life, I can tell you that."

When he had finished his interview with the Superintendent, Mr Akroyd went to find Gavin, who was poring over an ordnance survey map, as he did hour after hour.

"What's all this about that female?" Mr Akroyd demanded without preliminaries.

"What female?" Gavin said warningly. "If you mean Emma Ruskin—"

139

"This bloke Moss seems to think she'd got something to do with it. Is that right? If you and Jean between you have brought some criminal into my house and put my little girl in danger—"

"She's not a criminal."

"Oh, and how would you know, Mr Smartarse? I said all along Poppy should go to school. If she'd gone to school, none of this would have happened."

"She went to school and got ill – you know that, Dad. Emma's got nothing to do with it. Don't you realise she's in danger too? Probably more danger than Poppy. If they've got any sense they won't hurt Poppy, because they expect you to pay good money for her, but the same doesn't apply to—" His voice broke and failed him, The thought of what they might do to Emma was his worst nightmare, and something he didn't dare allow into his mind, or it would unfit him for anything.

Mr Akroyd softened, and laid a hand on his son's shoulder. "There, lad," he said gruffly. "She'll be all right. I dare say you're right, and she's got nothing to do with it. It's all fallen on you, this, hasn't it?"

"I feel so helpless," Gavin said bleakly. "If only there was something I could do."

Mr Akroyd nodded sympathetically. "Aye, well, the police are onto it. We just have to let them do their job."

Superintendent Moss came in looking a little more cheerful. "Now we're getting a fix on them! The post office says the ransom note was posted in Hockwold – that's a little village about fifteen miles away on the edge of the fens—"

"Yes, I know it," Gavin said.

"You do?"

"I know the fens and the forest very well. I've ridden for miles all over the area," he said shortly. There had been many, many days when he had needed to get away from the tensions and humiliations of home; and from horseback you saw the country – like your own problems – much more clearly.

"Right," said Moss. "And we've found the stolen Rover dumped on the back road between Hockwold and Feltwell. We've also got a car reported stolen in Weeting, which is about the same distance from Hockwold, but on the other side."

"What's that got to do with us?" Mr Akroyd asked impatiently.

"Bear with me," Moss said, and led them over to the table where Gavin's map was spread out. "You see, I think they've realised they can't get petrol for the Rover without giving themselves away, so Chummy, the driver, has been told to post the ransom letter, dump the Rover, and steal something else, but not all in the same place. Feltwell to Weeting is about seven miles by road or, say, five across country. Two hours on foot. He drives to Hockwold, posts the letter, drives on towards Feltwell until the petrol runs out, and then – this is the really cunning bit in his tiny mind – doubles back on himself before he steals the new motor. That way he thinks we'll never connect the two."

Gavin stared. "Can he really be that stupid?"

"You'd be surprised," Moss said feelingly, "how stupid the average criminal is. Good thing too, or we'd never catch 'em."

"But if he'd stolen the new car before he posted the letter, he could have posted it a lot further away," Gavin pointed out.

"Well, evidently he didn't think of that," Moss said. "I wonder, though, what his boss is going to have to say about it."

"His boss?" Mr Akroyd queried sharply.

"Chummy didn't plan the thing – he's too dim for that. I reckon he's just the driver – the muscles. Someone with a bit more nous is behind it. And that someone's not going to be too happy that Chummy posted the letter so close to home."

141

"Home?"

"Feltwell is about twelve miles from Pratchett's Wood where the Rover was stolen, and the Rover had very little petrol in it – only about ten miles' worth, the owner says. Well, there's always a bit more in the tank than you think, but not much. So the place where they've got the hostages stashed can't be far from Pratchett's Wood."

"But now they've got a new car," Gavin said, "they can move them again. They could be anywhere by now."

"I don't think so," Moss said. "In my view, the plan would have been to hole up in some deserted place, an isolated house, hidden in a wood maybe. The house would have to have been chosen and prepared beforehand, so I don't think they'll lightly abandon it. The more you drive your victims around the country the more likely you are to be spotted. No, I think they'll stick as close to their original plan as possible. The place they've chosen must be well hidden, and they'll be confident we won't find it."

He sounded so smug that Mr Akroyd gave him a sharp look. "Are you on to something? If so, spit it out, man! Have you got something you haven't told us yet?"

Moss smiled triumphantly. "Yes, we've got a pretty good idea who we're dealing with. As I said before, the driver of the car's a stupid man, luckily for us. He's also a heavy smoker. OK, every kid burglar these days knows enough to wear gloves, and there've been no finger-prints on the van or the dumped car – everything wiped clean. But on the floor of the Rover we found an empty cigarette pack and the cellophane wrapper from a new pack. The old pack is clean, but there's a beautiful set of nice greasy fingermarks on the cellophane." He positively grinned at Gavin, who, using his imagination, got the point at once.

"He finished a pack," Gavin said, "threw it down, tried to open a new pack, found he couldn't get the wrapper off with gloves on—"

"And took them off!" Mr Akroyd finished, getting there half a second behind.

"Exactly," Moss said. "We've run them through the computer and found they belong to an old chum of ours, Andrew Joseph Luckmeed. Got a record as long as your arm. The interesting thing about him is he's not long out of Blundeston, finished a stretch there in February. And while he was inside, he was keeping very close company with one Henry Gordon James, a felon very well known to us for various kinds of criminal activity. Gentleman Jim, he's known as, owing to his ability to put on a posh accent and mingle with the nobs on their own terms. And Harry James, alias Gentleman Jim, finished his last stretch in April – came out and promptly disappeared."

"You think he's the brains behind this?" Mr Akroyd asked. "Why? Has he done this sort of thing before?"

"Not kidnapping, no. Fraud, protection, gun-running, large-scale burglary, he's had his fingers in all of them. But he's always been one for elaborate plans – that's what lets him down. And snatching a little kid who couldn't fight back would be just up his alley. It'd look like easy money; and he's getting to the age when he'll be wanting to go for the big one and retire on the proceeds to Argentina. They all dream of it, your 'master criminals'." He invested the words with a world of contempt. "Moreover, he's a local lad, grew up in Thetford, first got into trouble as a teenager knocking off stuff from the base at Lakenheath. So he knows the area. All in all, I'm confident he's our man, all right."

On the evidence, Gavin was inclined to agree with him. "So, if it is this man, do you think – I mean, he doesn't sound too dangerous?" he said hopefully. "He's not likely to do anything violent, is he?"

Moss's face grew grave. "I don't want to frighten you. But I wouldn't want you to think this man's a soft option.

No, he's a cold-blooded bastard, like all these habituals; and the only violence he'd want to avoid is violence to himself. He's dangerous all right." He made an obvious effort to be cheerful. "But we'll get him, don't you worry."

Chapter Twelve

Gavin had pored over the map so often that its details were now engraved on his mind. The area they had now marked down as likely was a fairly unpopulated one, most of it in the Thetford Forest and the Hockwold fens: woodland, scrub and bog, a few scattered villages and farms and very few roads.

"It's narrowing down very nicely," Superintendent Moss said. "Obviously their hideout has got to be an isolated house, where they can come and go without being seen. Nosy neighbours would be no good to them. You can't shift two struggling prisoners up the front path of a council estate semi without being noticed."

"True," said Gavin.

"And that gives us about ten possibles. It's a matter of having a look at them and making discreet enquiries." He tapped the map thoughtfully. "Meanwhile, of course, we've got other lines to follow up."

"I suppose you mean Emma's past history?" Gavin said hotly. His father snapped an enquiring look at him, which was not lost on the Superintendent.

"Oh, we've gone into that, sir," Moss said easily. "Talked to her flat-mates, her previous headmistress, and her mum and dad. Well, we'd have had to let them know what'd happened anyway. Pretty upset, they are. Seem very nice people. Not what you'd expect."

"What does that mean?" Gavin snapped.

"Oh, nothing against the girl," Moss said. "No, she checks

145

out clean as a whistle. But it's a long way from where she started to a place like this." He waved his hand to indicate the handsome house and large park, taking in by implication the antiques, paintings, servants, cars and stables on the way.

Mr Akroyd, still watching Gavin's face, said quietly, "Come to that, Superintendent, it's a long way from where *I* started to a place like this."

The Superintendent coughed. "Quite so, Mr Akroyd. Yes, indeed. Well," he went on hastily, "if it wasn't Miss Ruskin, and it wasn't any of the servants – which we're pretty sure it wasn't – I'm at a bit of a loss to know who the inside contact was. I don't suppose either of you has any further suggestions?"

Mr Akroyd shook his head; Gavin's face was a careful blank.

The day dragged by. On one of Andy's visits, Emma tried to get talking to him, hoping perhaps to get him onto their side.

"What are you doing mixed up in something like this? You don't seem such a bad bloke, really," she said.

He looked at her unsmilingly. "Thank you very much, princess," he said. "Whajjer think I'm in it for? The money, of course. That's what we all want, ennit?"

"Don't you have any conscience about it?"

He eyed her derisively. "What do you care if her old man has to flog a few shares to get her back? Why should he have money and me none?"

Poppy looked up fiercely at that. "My father earned that money! He started off with nothing and earned every penny of it! What've you ever done?"

He only laughed at her. "Go it, Arry mate! What I done is I got you. I don't want you – he does. He's got money. I ain't. Fair swap, ennit?"

"You won't get away with it!" Poppy cried.

He grew bored with the conversation. "Oh shut your

146

mouth! You talk too much, both of you," he said, waving his gun at them idly. "I'll give you a friendly warning – keep it zipped when the Boss comes to see you. He ain't a patient man like me. If you start rabbitting on at him like that, you might get something you don't like."

"Is he coming to see us?" Emma asked, suddenly afraid.

Andy saw her fear, and grinned, enjoying it. "Yeah, later today. Summink to look forward to, ain't it, princess?"

The Boss's visit was short and chilling.

"We haven't had the response we wanted from the kid's dad," he said without preamble. "I'm afraid he's not taking us seriously, so we're going to have to send him a little something to concentrate his mind. Andy?" He held out his hand for the gun. Andy passed it over and then pulled something out from his pocket. There was a click, and a thin, viciously sharp blade appeared in his hand. He started to approach them, and Poppy screamed and flung herself into Emma's arms.

"No!" Emma cried, clutching the child against her. Poppy started sobbing with terror. "Don't you touch her, you monster!"

"Shaddap!" the Boss shouted. "Bloody women! Shut your noise. He wants a bit of her hair, that's all. Let her go. Get to the other end of the bed where I can see you. Move it, or I'll put one through your leg and see how you like that. Move it, I say! I've got no brief to keep you in one piece."

Reluctantly, keeping one eye on Andy and the other on the gun, Emma detached Poppy's arms from her neck. The child sobbed louder, and Andy suddenly said, "It's all right, kid. I only want a bit of your hair. Tell her, princess."

In terror the two of them watched the glittering blade approach Poppy's head; Emma knew there was nothing she could do to protect her, and yet every instinct screamed at her to fight. Andy grabbed a loose hank of Poppy's hair. Poppy screamed again. The knife flashed, and then Andy was stepping back with the knife in one hand and a hank of thin blonde hair in the other. Poppy began to sob again, but at a lower pitch, putting her hands up to her head. Emma gathered her in again, watching the two men like a cornered fox.

The Boss surveyed the two of them with eyes of utter cold indifference. "This goes in the second letter. If there has to be a third letter, it won't be hair, it'll be a finger."

Poppy cried out, and pressed so hard against Emma, it was as if she were trying to burrow her way in. Emma folded her arms round the child's head fiercely. "Go away! Leave us alone!" she cried uselessly. The two men went, locking the door as always, but she could not think it was on her command. When they were alone again, she and Poppy both burst into tears; and cried their eyes out for ten minutes or more, after which they curled up together on the bed and fell into an uneasy doze.

Zara looked up as Gavin came into her room. She was pale, nervous and distinctly guilty, and she took refuge in attack as the best form of defence. "Can't you knock? Get out of here. This is my own private room."

"You can talk to me here, or you can talk to me in front of Dad – take your pick," he said, closing the door and standing in front of it with his arms folded.

"I've got nothing to say to you," she snapped. "Get out."

"Zara, you know something about this. I know you do. I've known you all your life, and you've got guilt written all over you. Now you tell me what it is, or I go to Dad, and he and the police can get it out of you."

"I don't know what you're talking about," she said, but her eyes slid away from him.

He let his voice soften a little. "Don't be a little idiot. For God's sake, they've got Poppy! Your own sister. I don't expect you to care particularly what happens to Emma—"

Zara's eyes flashed. "Oh, Emma is it now? That little

tramp's had her eye on you since the minute she arrived. I knew what her game was the moment I saw her—"

Gavin crossed the room in three swift strides and grabbed Zara by the upper arms, and shook her. "It's your game I'm interested in! What do you know about this business?"

"Nothing! Let me go!" She tried to turn her face away from him, but he grabbed her jaw and turned it back.

"Look at me! Tell me!"

"It wasn't my fault. I didn't know what he wanted," she said, her eyes darting. She saw his expression change and grew genuinely frightened. "It was a bit of fun, that's all. We went to this club—"

"Who's we?"

"Vic and Nat and me."

"What club?"

"Bunter's. In Cambridge. It was just a bit of fun."

An expression of distaste crossed his face. He knew Bunter's – loud, noisy, and filled with rough youths and sluttish girls. "Slumming," he said in a flat voice. He let her go. "I suppose that gives you a thrill."

"You needn't look like that," she said, rubbing her arms where he had gripped her. "It's something different to do, that's all. It's all right for you – you're a man. I never have any fun. I'm always supposed to go out with 'nice' boys. Well, nice boys are boring, let me tell you. And stuck away here in the middle of nowhere, it had to be nice boys, 'cos they're the only ones who have cars."

"That's why you kept nagging at Dad for a car," Gavin said. "I knew it was a bad idea."

"Well, I got one, anyway, so there's nothing you can do about it."

"How did you get to the club before?"

"Vic's dad's car. Well, he never knew. He was never bloody well there."

"Don't swear. You're just adding to your sins."

"Sins!" she jeered.

149

"And crimes. Driving without insurance, and without the owner's permission. I don't suppose you'd want the police to know about that."

"I'd only get a fine," she muttered, "and Mummy'd pay it."

"Tell me about this man," Gavin said. His eyes were cold and remote, and they frightened her rather. "What was his name?"

"Billy Metcalf. I met him at the club. He came up to me, said was I Zara Akroyd. He said he'd seen my photo in *Country Life*."

"When was this?"

"Ages ago, the first time. Last year – September or October. I – I didn't like him at first. He was a bit of a tough, if you want to know. But there was something about him. Kind of scary. He wasn't like the dorky men we usually get to meet. He bought us drinks, and we danced a bit, and he chatted. Then he asked if he could drive me home, and I said no. And that was that."

"Go on."

"The next time was a couple of weeks later. He came up to me again, like before; then I started bumping into him at other places. Well, I was bored stiff so I let him hang around with me. Vic and Nat were wild about him. They said they betted he was a crim. I kept asking if he had any friends for them. But actually, it wasn't as exciting as they thought. Mostly he wanted to talk, about the house, and Mummy, and what Dad did, and all that kind of thing. He never even wanted to fool around or anything. He only kissed me once, and that was—" She paused, remembering it. It had not been pleasant, not romantic or sexy or anything. He had kissed her as if he knew she was expecting it and it simply amused him to give her something she wanted, but that he knew she wouldn't like. It was a kiss like an insult.

Gavin could see it all. "And when did you bring him here?"

150

She flushed. "Just before Easter. Dad was in Sunderland and you'd gone to Exeter about that legal case, and Mummy was taking Poppy to see the specialist in London, and Mrs H went up with them so there was nobody here. Billy'd been on at me for ages to take him to my home. He told me to let him know when there'd be no one around – gave me a telephone number. I thought he wanted—" Her blush deepened. Gavin's lips tightened. "Well, anyway," she went on, "he didn't want anything like that. He wanted to see over the house. I showed him everything. He was really interested. He seemed to know a lot about buildings and stuff." She caught Gavin's expression and hurried on. "And he asked about my birthday party as well. Wanted to know every detail of what was going to happen on the day. I thought—" her eyes suddenly filled with tears, "I thought he was going to buy me a birthday present, something really expensive. I hinted like mad for a few things I fancied and he seemed to take it in. He said – he said he was planning a real surprise for me. I knew I'd never be allowed to invite him officially, so I told him how he could get in through the boot room. I said if he wore a DJ no one'd know."

"Oh my God, Zara!"

She gulped. "But after that visit I never saw him again, and when I rang the number he'd given me, it was discontinued. And then when the police said there must have been inside information for the kidnapping, I realised—"

Gavin closed his eyes wearily. "You've behaved like an absolute idiot, you know that."

"It wasn't my fault," she said with spirit. "It's all right for you, you can do what you like. I'm always told I can't do this and I can't do that. Everyone's on my back. I never have any fun. I just wanted a bit of fun."

Gavin held his tongue. There was no point in telling her off. It was done now. "You'll have to come and tell all this to Superintendent Moss."

"No! It's my own private business."

"Yes! You fool, don't you see if they can find this Billy Metcalf, he can lead them to the kidnappers?" Still she resisted. "If you don't come this instant," he said in a hard voice, "I'll carry you down there."

She got up sulkily. "Are you going to tell Dad?"

"He'll have to know. But at the moment, he's only interested in getting Poppy back."

She managed one last sneer. "And your precious Emma."

"I hope so. Oh God, I hope so."

"We've got him," Superintendent Moss said, putting down the phone. "He was hanging around one of his usual haunts. So confident we'd never find out he had anything to do with it, he didn't even go into hiding. He's an old friend of Harry James — if 'friend' is the right word. Anyway, he's been to see him a few times at Blundeston. The way I see it, he stumbled on Zara at this club, realised who she was, and cultivated her friendship while he told Harry about it and waited for him to work out some way of using the contact."

"You still think Harry James is the master-mind?"

"Oh yes. Billy Metcalf is no thinker. His part was to provide the initial information; and I suspect he was watching the drop site as well, so he could tell James when the money was there." Moss rubbed his hands with satisfaction. "Now we've just got to get out of him where the hideout is."

"Let me have ten minutes alone with him, and I'll get it out of him," Mr Akroyd growled.

"If we were allowed to use those methods, we'd get it out of him ourselves," Moss said. "Unfortunately there's such a thing as the PACE Act. But we'll put the pressure on him other ways."

"Meanwhile, we sit here and twiddle our thumbs?" Mr Akroyd said. "That second letter—"

Moss looked sympathetic. "Yes, it's an unusual situation. Kidnappers generally like to talk about it on the 'phone,

152

and that gives you a chance to argue. Doing it by post is most unusual, and it ties our hands a bit. We can't tell them we're getting the money but it'll take time, or demand proof that the hostages are still all right, or any of the usual dodges to keep them busy. But that takes nerve on their side. Gentleman Jim must be very confident this time. We've got to find them, to be able to take any action—"

"Well, find them!" Akroyd suddenly shouted. "Bloody find them!"

"We're doing our best, sir," Moss said courteously.

"I've got an idea," Gavin said tentatively. "About where the hideout might be."

The Superintendent looked up receptively. "Let's have it, then."

It was early in the morning. No one had slept. Billy Metcalf certainly hadn't, but he was still resisting the questioning.

"I was going over the map again," Gavin went on, spreading it out on the table, "and thinking, how would these people have got hold of a house? It would have to have been for sale or to let, and if they've only been planning it since October, they couldn't have banked on the right sort of house just happening to come empty at the right time."

"Go on," Moss nodded.

"There's a place, about *here*—" He put his finger down on the map. "I know it from my riding expeditions. It's a house called Sparlings." Moss looked down, and then up, enquiringly. "No, it's not marked. It was empty for years because it was supposed to be haunted, and then the Forestry Commission bought the land and the house with it, and it's just been let go. I don't know what condition it's in now, but when I last saw it, about a year ago, or a bit more, it was still in reasonable shape. I mean, it had a roof and walls and doors, though most of the windows were broken. You could live in it, if you weren't too particular. There wouldn't be

153

any electricity or water, of course, but it had a well in the garden, and a person could always take a camp stove to boil the water on."

"Hmm," Moss pondered. "And Harry James is a local man . . ."

"So he'd be bound to know about it," Gavin said, following the thought. "When I was a kid it was a 'dare' place for boys, because of being haunted. And older lads used to go there to smoke or mess about."

"I think you've got something," Moss said. "We'd better take a look at this Sparlings place. In fact, I think I'll go myself."

"Please – let me go with you!" Gavin begged, his eyes naked. He needed so desperately to do something. The waiting and the inactivity were torture.

Moss smiled. "I was thinking of it," he said. "I need you to show me where it is, apart from anything else. But listen to me," the smile disappeared. "No heroics, you understand? You stick close to me, do nothing but what you're told to do: these people are dangerous. Above all you *say* nothing, no matter what the provocation. Keep your mouth shut, and your eyes and ears open, and tell me afterwards if you notice anything. Agreed?"

"Agreed," said Gavin.

Sparlings stood amongst trees, and what had once been its garden was overgrown with brambles and ivy. By the time Gavin and Moss arrived with two uniformed constables, three other officers were already in place, hidden in the trees and bushes: one at the front and two at the back.

The man watching the front of the house made room for them silently. "All right, Gardner? Anything?" Moss asked.

Gardner removed the field-glasses from his face and handed them to Moss. "There's someone in there all right. I saw a movement at one of the upstairs windows about ten minutes ago. Nothing since."

"No sign of the hostages?"

"No, sir."

"No idea how many of 'em are in there?"

"No, sir."

"Hmm," said Moss. "You don't know much, and that's a fact." He surveyed the house closely. Gavin looked too, with his unaided sight. The windows of the ground floor had been boarded up, but the upstairs windows had been reglazed since he had last seen the place. It was a simple, square house – rather like a child's drawing, with a window at each corner and a door in the middle, a pointed roof and a chimney. An old and very thick creeper grew over the face of it, and there was a tumbledown collection of sheds and lean-tos to one side. Round to the rear, as Gavin knew from his past explorations, there was another short wing to the house, making it effectively an L-shape cradling a small yard at the back, with more sheds and old stables.

At last the Superintendent lowered the binoculars. "All right," he said, "I think I'll go and have a word with them."

"Sir—" Gardner said, in warning or protest. Moss looked at him impatiently. "It could be dangerous. They might be armed, sir. Why not go in in force, take 'em on all sides at once? We can get the Armed Response Unit here in fifteen minutes, no sweat. Overpower 'em before they've got a chance to make plans."

Moss looked pained. "No, no, no. Let that lot in with their hormones on the rampage? D'you want to start a shoot-out? I don't want bullets flying around when we don't know exactly where the hostages are. Besides, we don't know yet that we've got the right place. Let's find out what we're dealing with first. The whole thing could be legit, and then we'd look like prize prawns, sending the ARU in against a bunch of woolly squatters."

He stepped out of the shelter of the bushes and looked the house over carefully.

155

"I still think it would be better to try and take 'em by surprise," Gardner tried one last protest.

"Too late for that, laddie," Moss said, seeing a movement at a window. "They already know we're here."

He turned to his uniformed companions. "All right, Simpson, Clarke, come with me. The rest of you keep out of sight. Yes, all right, Mr Akroyd, you can come too. Stick close and keep your mouth shut – remember what I told you."

Gavin nodded, and the four of them started out towards the front door. "Let's keep it nice and relaxed," Moss said as they neared the house. "We don't want anybody frightened into doing anything rash." And he stepped into the porch and rapped on the door. Gavin pointed out the old-fashioned iron bell-pull, and he pulled on that, too, and they heard the bell ringing somewhere in the depths of the house.

Gavin didn't think they would get any response, and was surprised when after only a short delay the door was opened. Before them stood a middle-aged man with close-cropped grey hair, a lined, pale face, and very watchful eyes behind wire-rimmed glasses. He was dressed in grey trousers and a white shirt without a tie. He looked neat and tidy, but tired and unwell. Seeing him standing there, apparently unarmed, and the bare house open behind him, Gavin wanted to rush him, grab him, pin him to the wall and make him tell them where Poppy and Emma were. Behind him he almost felt the uniformed officers stir, as if they, too, felt the same urge.

But Superintendent Moss was a monument of calm. "Well, well, well," he said with cold geniality. "If it isn't Gentleman Jim! And what might you be doing here, may I ask?"

"Hullo, Superintendent," the man said without pleasure. "I was about to ask you the same thing."

"I asked first," Moss insisted.

"I'm a local. Born and bred in Thetford. Why shouldn't I be here?"

"Just answer the question."

James shrugged. "I got to live somewhere. I've just come out of gaol, as no doubt you're aware." Moss nodded impassively. "I've got no money, nothing to live on, and I knew this house was empty, so – I sought shelter. Everyone's got the right to basic shelter, haven't they?"

"Every honest man, maybe."

James managed to look pained. "I hope you aren't going to harass me, Superintendent. I've paid my debt to society. I'm a respectable law-abiding member of the public now."

"Haven't laid a finger on you," Moss said smoothly. "Yet. On your own here, are you?"

"Of course. Who were you expecting?"

"We're looking for a friend of yours. Andy Luckmeed."

"I haven't seen him. I told you, I'm only just out."

"He came to see you in gaol, Harry. We know that."

"I haven't seen him since I came out. What d'you want him for?"

"Broken his parole. Hasn't checked in. Don't want the lad to get in trouble, do we?"

James looked past Moss's shoulder at the uniformed men. "All this just to look for a missing parolee? What are you up to, Moss?"

"*Mr* Moss, if you don't mind. Well, if Andy's not here, and you're not up to anything, you won't mind if we come in and have a look round, will you?"

Gavin was aware of the increase in tension in the Superintendent as he put this question. But James did not flinch, or whip out a gun, or take to his heels. He merely smiled – a slow, spreading, unpleasant smile.

"Not at all," said Gentleman James silkily. "Be my guest. I'm sorry I can't offer you anything, but I'm living here under rather Spartan conditions."

He stepped back and extended his arm, inviting them past him; Moss's face was far from happy as he walked in.

*   *   *

157

Climbing into the back of the police car beside Gavin, Moss said, "Smartarse little bastard! I'd like to take him to pieces!" He fumed for a moment or two in silence, and then asked Gavin, "Did you see anything?"

"There was nothing to see, was there?" Gavin said, depressed.

"I knew there wouldn't be, or he wouldn't have asked us in." He shook his head again. "Bastard! He must've moved 'em. I suppose Andy Luckmeed's got 'em holed up somewhere else. Damn it, now we've got to start again from scratch."

"Can't you arrest him, make him tell us?"

Moss shook his head. "Nothing to arrest him for. I've got nothing to connect him to the snatch except that he knows Luckmeed and Metcalf — but so do lots of people."

"But he's trespassing, isn't he? Can't you get him for that?"

"He's squatting, and to get him out I have to have a court order proving criminal damage."

"But—"

"It wouldn't make him any more likely to tell us where he's stashed 'em, would it? No, no, we need him on the loose, so that he can give himself away and lead us to them. He was very bold, showing us round, Mr Harry James — very confident, but he wasn't happy about it. He knows we'll be watching his every move now. He thought we'd never find him in a deserted house in the middle of a wood, and he must have been pig-sick when we turned up at the door. If we keep the pressure up, he'll panic and give himself away, or make a break for it. Then we've got him."

"And if he doesn't?"

"Well, to get the money he's got to communicate with one of his mates, hasn't he? And they're not over-endowed with brains. They're his weak spots — them, and his own over-confidence."

But meanwhile, Gavin thought, Poppy and Emma are

158

in danger, frightened and alone. There must be some way he could help them. And there was something about the house that was bothering him. He didn't know what, but something.

Chapter Thirteen

Andy, going idly to the window to see what sort of day it was, had seen Moss and his companions arrive. He sprang back from the window like a scalded cat, and then rushed to the Boss's room.

"The cops are outside! There's a police car! They're coming to the door!" he babbled. "What're we gonna do, Boss? Shoot it out?"

The Boss was just finishing shaving, with difficulty, in a tiny bowl before a hand-mirror propped on the dado-rail. He scowled. "*Shoot it out*? What's the matter with you? Pull yourself together, for God's sake! You've got a brain like a colander."

"A what?" Andy said blankly.

"Skip it. I've told you we're quite safe here. What I'm going to do is invite them in—"

"*What*?" Andy almost shrieked.

"Shut up! I'll keep them talking at the door for as long as possible, but then I shall invite them in. They'll look round, and they'll find nothing, and then they'll leave."

"But Boss—!"

"Don't you see, you idiot, it's the only way to convince them we haven't got the kid here? They've got nothing on us. They can't touch us. What you're going to do is go to the room, lock yourself in with 'em, and keep 'em quiet at all costs. You'd better gag them – the girl is capable of risking getting shot for the sake of getting the kid rescued." He said it without admiration. "If there's no other choice, cold cock 'em, but try not to damage the kid. When it's all clear, I'll come and knock."

Emma and Poppy had still been asleep when Andy came in, which allowed him to get the gag on her before she really knew what was happening.

"Sit there on the bed," he told her, "put your hands on your head; don't move an inch, or make a sound, or I'll belt the kid with this." He gestured with the gun. Emma stared at him, eyes wide and confused above the gag.

"What're you going to do to us?" Poppy whispered, her eyes filling with tears of fear.

"Shut up," Andy snapped. "I'm not going to hurt you. Now turn around."

He turned her with a rough hand on her shoulder, and gagged her too. Emma's mind was clearing. There's someone out there, she thought. Someone's come to the house – the police? Someone's traced us, and if I don't do something they'll go away and never know we were here. She stood up, regardless of the danger, but Andy took a step forward, gun raised, his face pulled into an ugly sneer.

"Don't even think it! You make one false move, princess, and I'll knock you out. D'you want another head wound? Sit down, hands on your head. *Sit down!*"

Emma sat, miserably, on the edge of the bed, and Andy thrust Poppy down on her knees in front of and facing Emma, effectively blocking any movement.

"That goes for you too, Arry," he said, rubbing the muzzle of the gun against the side of Poppy's face to get her attention. "You move or make a sound, and I'll hit *her*, right where she got it before. You get me? Now *shut up!*"

They waited, Emma sitting, Poppy kneeling and pressed against her knees, Andy standing behind Poppy and holding her by her hair. Tears rolled freely down Poppy's face, soaking the gag. Andy was braced and taut, listening, sweating rankly with fear. Emma listened too, her heart thumping like a trapped bird in her chest, hoping and fearing.

161

Oh find us, please find us! she thought desperately. There were footsteps and bumps, now near, now far, now on the floor above their heads. *We're here*, she cried in her mind, willing them to come, trying to call them telepathically. But after a long time, the footsteps went away, and eventually perfect silence reigned. And then there was a knocking on the door, which made them all jump. But Andy sighed with relief, and she knew it was not rescue.

"All clear," he said, backing to the door and taking the key out of his pocket. He unlocked it, and the Boss came in, looking pleased with himself.

"Well, that's that," he said. His hard eyes met Emma's above her gag. "The police have been here – in force, I may add. They've been here, searched the house to their hearts' content, and gone away again, perfectly satisfied that you aren't here, and never have been. Brains, you see, will always overcome brawn." He grinned. "Your would-be rescuers stood only feet from you, and walked away again."

Poppy was crying dismally, and Emma stared at their tormentor with hatred. He didn't need to come and say those things. He did it because he wanted to hurt them. He didn't just want the money. He wanted power over people, and when he had that power, he would use it to be cruel. She realised then that they had been lucky so far not to be hurt; that luck might not hold in the future. If the money was not forthcoming, he might very well want to prove himself by taking it out on them. Her heart sank to its lowest level yet. Did the police really think they had never been here? Did that mean there was no chance of rescue?

The Boss seemed happy with his effect on them. "All right, Andy, you can take the gags off. Then lock 'em in and come with me."

The Boss left, and Andy undid Poppy's gag. She dragged in some sobbing breaths, and Andy, seeming a little unnerved by her crying, said, "Oh, can it, kid! Nobody's hurting you,

162

are they? As soon as your old man coughs up the dough, you'll be home and dry."

"He'll *never* pay you!" Poppy sobbed passionately. "Daddy won't give you a *penny!*"

"You'd just better hope he does," Andy said grimly. "I reckon you can manage for yourself, princess." Emma undid the gag, and he held out his hand for it impassively, and then went away, banging the door behind him. Poppy flung herself into Emma's arms, and Emma let her have her cry out. When the child was calm again, Emma got up and went over to the corner, took the handkerchief out of her pocket and poked it through the hole in the wall. There was a saying about stable doors and horses; but there was just an outside chance that someone might come back. And in any case, there was nothing else she could do.

Gavin wandered round in a fret of anxiety. Something about the house bothered him, but what? It nagged and nagged at him senselessly; like the sound of a baby crying in the distance, it was something he couldn't quite ignore, and yet which he could do nothing about.

The police had their duties to follow, leaning on Billy Metcalf, looking for Andy Luckmeed, trying to prove a recent connection between them and Harry James, searching for any clue as to where the hostages had been moved to — and how. But Gavin, with nothing to do to occupy him, just went over and over the situation in his head, retreading in imagination the bare floorboards of that house, seeing again the dusty rooms, empty but for dead leaves and bits of fallen plaster. The search had been thorough enough to satisfy even him that Poppy and Emma were not there.

But what, he asked himself, was Sparlings for, if it was not where they had taken the victims? Why would James go to the trouble of setting up the house just for himself, while his prisoners were kept somewhere else? Logic had led the searchers to Sparlings, a logic which said the gang needed an isolated place, and a place they knew would be empty. How many more such were there within the area? Why hadn't the police, who had been methodically visiting every isolated house, found it by now?

No, Sparlings must have been meant as the hideout. But if that were so, why would they move the prisoners elsewhere? And when? They could not have done it when the police first arrived: the house had been surrounded, and no one had come out. And if they did it *before* the police arrived – well, why? You were back to *why*? It made no sense.

Yet Harry James had been so utterly confident that they would find nothing; his confidence, and the fruitless search, had convinced Superintendent Moss. But Gavin's mind would not rest. Logic said the prisoners must be in the house; and if that were the case, they must be hidden in some particularly clever way. Yes, Harry James was pleased with himself – pleased with his cleverness. The prisoners were there, but James was sure they would never find them.

The only thing to do, he thought, was to go back and have another look. The police wouldn't do it, of course. They were pursuing their own plan. But there was nothing – except the police themselves – to prevent Gavin from breaking in at night and taking a look around. As soon as he came to the decision, a great calmness came over him. He was going to take action at last; and it was the right thing to do. He knew they were in there somewhere.

When the house was quiet, he got up, dressed in black trousers and a black roll-neck sweater, put on soft-soled black moccasins. He put his Swiss army knife into his pocket, and a pencil torch and a short but very heavy spanner into the other pocket. On a thought he added a plastic card with which to slip any Yale lock he might encounter. Then he went quietly down the back stairs and out into the park. The moon was in its first quarter, but it was a clear night, so there was enough light to see by.

He had moved his car during the day, leaving it near the side gate to the park, which he had left unlocked. He drove as near as he dared to the place, and then left his car and walked the rest. He had the advantage that he knew the ground and he knew where the police were positioned. The officers had made a loose perimeter round the house, but they would be looking for someone to break out, not to break in. And with all his experience of badger-watching and bird-watching, Gavin could move as soundlessly as a cat.

His object was a small window in the side of the house facing onto the back yard. Once you got up to it, it was hidden from view by a jutting-out corner of brickwork, and it gave onto one of the old pantries, the inside door of which was not lockable. As long as it hadn't been nailed up – and he saw no reason why it should have been – he would be able to get into the rest of the house from there.

Nearing the house, he looked up at the sky, and then hunkered down amongst the bushes to wait. There was a swathe of clouds moving across the sky, which in five or ten minutes would obscure the moon. It would then be quite dark. He had only to wait. It was very unlikely that he would be seen – but if he was, what could they do? They couldn't shoot him, or even shout at him. They could only wait for him to come out again – and he didn't mind if they grabbed him after he came out.

The cloud shadow came up; the moon disappeared. In the blackness Gavin rose and ran quickly and silently across the open space and into the shelter of the house wall, and crept along it to the window. There he stood, listening. Everything was silent, inside and out. Good!

There was a board over the window, but it didn't take him long with his knife to prise the nails out of the rotten wood and set the board aside. Behind it the window was totally innocent of glass: many a boy had wriggled in this way, he thought, over the years – he had done so himself. He thanked God that he was slim, and agile: he hoisted himself up, squeezed through, and dropped lightly to the floor in the empty pantry. The pantry door was not nailed up: it yielded to a push, and he opened it a crack, listened, opened it a little further, and finally slipped out into the empty kitchen passage.

There he stopped and listened again. The house was in silence, except for the pounding in his ears of his own heart. He stood still, breathing slowly and deeply until he was calm again; and then, all his senses on the stretch, he began his search.

It was easier than he had thought it would be to eliminate rooms in which they could not be concealed. There were no cellars to the house, but he wondered whether some secret underground room might have been dug out by the villains for the purpose, though he thought it unlikely they could have managed that in the time available, and without attracting attention. However, he concentrated on looking for doors, concealed or new, which might lead to some underground space, or any door to any room which was locked or barred.

He found nothing. At the foot of the stairs he listened again, but the house was in silence. The stairs yawned before him, empty and menacing. He hesitated. His instincts feared a trap. Anything might be up there, waiting for him. As soon as he started up, he would be vulnerable. But then he thought of Emma. Suddenly she came into his mind, and it was like looking at a fragment of video film: he saw her as he had never seen her in life, turning over in bed with a little sigh as she stirred in her sleep. Was it just imagination, or was she here somewhere, had she just turned like that in real life, and in his heightened state of awareness he had somehow seen her do it? He shook the thoughts away. They were needlessly distracting. But they had cured his hesitation: he had come too far now to be put off. He started up, keeping close to the wall where there was less likelihood of the stairs creaking.

On the first floor there were closed doors and open doors leading off the landing. He chose the nearest open door. It was empty of furniture, and dark – darker than anywhere else in the house. He couldn't even see the outline of the window. Very cautiously, he put on his torch, aiming it at the floor. Dusty, naked floorboards. He advanced the beam slowly. No furniture, only bare boards and a cigarette butt trodden out on the floor. Bare white walls. Ah, that was why it was so dark in here – there was no window; only, on the far side, one of those huge, ugly Victorian wardrobes that often get left in houses when people move out because they won't fit in the new house. He remembered this room, now, from his earlier visit with Moss, remembered the wardrobe. They had looked inside it, of course, and found it empty.

Next to it, against the wall, was a rickety kitchen table; and on the floor under the table was something white. A piece of paper? Had it been there before? He couldn't remember. He crossed the room and picked it up. It was a handkerchief, ragged and torn. Was it a clue? Maybe. Maybe. He shoved it into his pocket, and was about to go when the thing that had been bothering him came up clearly into his mind at last. The room had no window. It was too large a room to be a cupboard: it was clearly a bedroom, but it had no window. That was not only odd, inexplicable, but he also knew that he had played in this house when he was a lad, and he didn't remember a windowless bedroom.

He looked at the wardrobe again. He didn't remember that being here when he was a lad, either. There hadn't been any furniture at all. Of course, someone could have moved it in at any time – there may well have been tramps or squatters here over the years – but a large wardrobe was an odd choice of furniture to bother with. He opened the door and glanced in, shining his torch, but it was still empty – not even a scrap of fluff.

167

Perhaps, he thought, the window was behind the wardrobe. It would be an odd thing to do, to put a wardrobe over the window, but the wall where it stood was the logical place in the room to *have* a window. He walked round the side of it and shone his torch. He didn't know what he had expected to see, but what he did see was that the wardrobe was absolutely flush with the wall, so close that not even a cigarette paper could have been slipped between. In fact, it looked as though it were part of the wall, joined to it like a built-in wardrobe.

Was this it? His heart was racing again, his palms sweating. He wiped them down his trouser legs. In doing so, he dropped the handkerchief, which he had not pushed into his pocket properly: the roughness of its torn surface caught on his fingers. He stooped to pick it up; and then, instead, flattened it out against the floorboards and shone his torch at it.

Through the white material the dark floorboards showed in the shape of frayed and crudely-cut letters, which seemed to shout at him like a shrill imperative – HELP POPPY!

They were here! He took another look at the wall and wardrobe, and understood everything. And now he must get out and get help, though every fibre of him wanted to tear the place apart with his bare hands. But he must do the sensible thing. He must not be caught now, when he had the information that was needed. His nerves were stretched to the limit, his hair was standing on end with the tension and the fear of being caught, and the adrenalin surging into his blood was screaming at him to run as fast as his legs could pump. It was the hardest thing he had ever had to do in his life, to make himself retrace his steps cautiously, quietly, slowly, on tiptoe, and without looking back. If the sound of his heart thudding didn't wake the villains, he thought, nothing would . . .

As soon as he reached the bushes, he was seized ungently by

168

two enormous pairs of hands. They must have seen him go in after all. Between them, two burly policemen bundled him hastily away from the house to a safe distance where they could bawl him out. He was not sorry for the support, since his own legs seemed to have gone temporarily on strike.

"You bloody idiot!" one of them hissed, so outraged he actually shook him. "What the hell did you think you were doing?"

Gavin had to search around for his voice, and when he found it, it didn't sound terribly like his.

"They're in there," he said. "I know where. I've got the proof."

"I should never have let you near the place," Superintendent Moss grumbled. "That's what comes of letting amateurs in on the game." But he didn't sound really put out about it. He had got his roaring over before Gavin came into his presence; and there was no doubt that Gavin's lunatic prank had advanced matters considerably.

"I realised that you couldn't be expected to break in," Gavin justified himself, "so I thought I'd do it for you. And besides, I know the house; I've been in it a hundred times."

"Well, as it happens, it's turned out all right, but you could have blown the whole thing, you know, and got yourself killed, to say nothing of your sister."

"I'm sure they didn't hear me. They'd have been down to find out what was going on if they'd heard anything."

"I won't ask where you learned your house-breaking skills, but you seem to have been lamentably professional about it," Moss said sternly. "But we must go carefully, now that we know your sister and Miss Ruskin are in there. What we don't want is for a hostage situation to develop, especially if they're armed. So no more unilateral action, all right, Mr Akroyd?"

"I promise you," Gavin said. "I'm no hero, and I wouldn't

169

do anything to put them in danger. What are you going to do now?"

"Get the armed units in position, and then try and talk them out."

"Please – you will let me come?"

"As long as I can trust you to stay out of the way."

"I promise."

"Right, then you may be useful. I may need you tell me the layout of the house."

And he waved Gavin away to get himself a cup of coffee, while he got on the telephone and started issuing instructions.

Chapter Fourteen

The Boss did not sleep well on a camp-bed. A good measure of Scotch got him off all right, but then he tended to wake after an hour or two and toss and turn the rest of the night, finally dropping off at about six and sleeping heavily until Andy woke him. He was in the tossing and turning stage of this annoying regime when he came suddenly full awake, and lay for a moment staring at the ceiling, frowning. Something had disturbed him, and he had learned during a misspent life not to ignore his instincts.

The dawn chorus was going on outside — was it that which had woken him? No, wait: the dawn chorus was general, but had fallen silent in the immediate vicinity of the house. And, yes, leafing through memory he dredged up the sharp *chack-chack-chack* alarm call of a blackbird: that was what had brought him to consciousness. Now all his senses were prickling. Something was going on out there.

He crawled stiffly out of bed (*never again*, he thought as he threw an evil glance at the thing) and, keeping out of line of sight, made his way to the window. He saw nothing unusual, but he knew all the same that something was happening. And after watching for some time he at last spotted a movement in the bushes, and caught a glimpse of the blue baseball cap with the black-and-white check band which could only belong to a police marksman.

He jumped back from the window and cursed long and fluently. He knew the form, and he knew that Moss would not have been able to turn out an armed unit without

171

convincing evidence that this was the right place. They were on to him, and in a big way. But what had given it away? He was sure Moss had been merely busking when he paid his visit here — though the Boss would have liked to know what brought the copper to this particular address in the first place. But Moss hadn't known that the kid and the girl were here when he first came — the Boss would have staked his reputation on that. Evidently some new information had come his way. It had to be Billy Metcalf, didn't it? The fool had got himself taken up and had given the game away. That must be it. The Boss cursed Metcalf, and indulged a brief dream of what he'd do to him when he got hold of it. That's what came of working with kids. The Boss had never trusted Metcalf, who was a loud-mouthed, flash little sod; but of course he'd had to bring him in after Metcalf tipped him off about the girl.

Well, there was no use crying about it now. He was dressing himself with quick, economical movements, his mind running ahead. The thing now was to get out, while the cops still thought they had the jump on him. He didn't want a shoot-out, particularly not with frustrated police marksmen, who yearned so much for the chance to pull the trigger they made Al Capone's gang look like the Salvation Army. Once it got to a siege, it was only a matter of time before you gave up or got shot, and the Boss had no intention of doing either. He was going to get away with the kid, and live to collect the loot. If necessary he'd shoot Andy and the other female: they were expendable. If they slowed him down, they were out, he thought, slipping his gun into the waistband of his trousers, and went to wake Andy.

"Come on you, get up, get some clothes on," he said, shaking him roughly.

"Wha? Whazza marra? Whassup?" Andy mumbled thickly, ungluing his eyes with difficulty. He was a revolting sight, the Boss thought dispassionately. God help anyone who had to rely on trash like this.

172

"Shut your mouth! The rozzers are outside. Billy must have blown us. Come on, get up! We've got to make a run for it."

Gavin was as tense as an overstrung violin as he waited with Superintendent Moss while the various police officers got themselves into position. They were highly-trained professionals, and they moved quietly, but there were so many of them, Gavin could not believe that the criminals inside hadn't been alerted. But the house remained quiet, and no faces showed at the windows.

Moss was checking the various units in on the radio link. Gavin thought about Poppy and Emma, and wondered if they were all right. Was Emma awake and wondering if she was going to be rescued? He imagined how frightened she must have been — probably still was, not knowing what was going to happen to her and Poppy. He tried to send her a thought wave: *Not long now. We're coming. Hold on.*

At last Superintendent Moss nudged Gavin and beckoned. "Come with me," he whispered.

"Is everyone in place?" Gavin asked.

"Nearly. I want you to come with me round the back and let me know any places you think they might make a break for it, any places we need to cover."

"OK."

"The place you broke in, for instance," Moss added with grim humour.

"Right. And what happens then? When everyone's in place?"

"We talk 'em out. There's a regular procedure for this sort of thing."

Gavin nodded. He'd seen it on the news and on films often enough. But in television dramas it never went right; someone always got killed. His mouth dry, he fell in behind Moss and they began to make their way round the house.

173

They had only gone half-way when there was a commotion from the back of the house: shouts, and a burst of gunfire. Moss's radio suddenly crackled into life. He clamped it to his ear.

"Damn it, they've made a run for it!" he shouted, breaking into a run. "Two of 'em, and the girls. Might be more still inside." And he shouted orders into the radio, for half the squad to close the circle round the house while the others pursued the fugitives.

The next few minutes seemed to Gavin a nightmare confusion of running and shouting. No one seemed to notice him. He simply stuck to the Superintendent, hoping no one would shoot him or turn him back. The man Harry James and another crook, with the hostages, had made a dash for it out of the back, shooting and wounding Simpson, who was just getting into position and had been in their way. Now they were running into the woods behind the house.

Alone, either of them could have got clean away, but the hostages were slowing them down. The Boss weighed the chances as they ran. He couldn't yet bring himself to abandon his scheme, his last hope for the Big Score; and besides, the police wouldn't fire on him while he had the kid as a shield. He jerked her along, and she stumbled again and almost tripped him. The wood was petering out up ahead, but there were too many people on their tails for them to run anywhere but straight on, up the slight slope and out of cover.

"Boss, let's dump 'em," Andy pleaded, panting. "We can make it on our own." He had charge of Emma, whose arms were once more tied. Every time she stumbled over her long dressing-gown, he hauled her upright by main force, which was exhausting to him and agonising to her.

"Don't be a fool," the Boss snapped. "D'you want to get shot? Without these two, we're sitting ducks." Poppy was white-faced, dazed, staggering like a zombie as he hauled at her arm; she'd have him down any minute. He stopped, grabbed her round the waist and hoisted her over his shoulder like a sack. But though small, she was a solid little kid, and he was not a fit man. His lungs laboured and his nerves screamed as he tried to keep his feet on the uneven, tussocky ground, hearing the police crashing through the undergrowth behind them like hunting dogs.

"'Sno use!" Andy gasped behind him. "We can't make it!"

The Boss knew he was right. Like flushed game they had been driven out of the trees and into the open, and running uphill they were losing ground. And there was nothing in front of them but more of the same, open country, no cover, nowhere to hide, no chance of stealing a car. It was over. The Boss saw his golden vision of comfortable retirement in the sun dissolve into the prospect a long gaol sentence – the discomfort, the smells, the squalor, the hopelessness. It was a last stand now, or nothing.

He stopped and turned in his tracks, swinging Poppy down from his shoulder onto her feet, and dragging her round in front of him, holding her round the throat with one arm while he drew his gun and thumbed off the safety. Andy, seeing the action, did likewise, taking stand beside him with Emma as his shield.

"Stand still!" the Boss shouted. "Stay where you are!"

The command was hardly needed. The police stopped as soon as they saw what was happening. They were a few yards off. Superintendent Moss, with Gavin still at his elbow, came through to the front of the line. The Boss waved his pistol to make sure they had seen it. "That's right, Mossy. Don't come any closer or the kid gets it," he said, putting the muzzle of the pistol against Poppy's right temple. Everyone froze.

Poppy drooped in the Boss's grip, looking dazed, as if she had only half an idea what was happening; but when her drifting gaze found Gavin, she stiffened and cried out "Gavin!" in a tone of desperate appeal. At the sound

175

of her voice Gavin's body jerked forward in automatic response, but the Boss made a savage gesture with the pistol and snarled, "You want some? You first, then the kid! I'm warning you! Moss, keep your dogs back. I'm not kidding."

Moss laid a hard hand on Gavin's arm, but Gavin had already stopped himself. He stared at the two men in front of him with horrified eyes. He couldn't believe this was happening.

"All right, Harry, take it easy," Moss said. He sounded amazingly calm, almost conversational, but Gavin beside him could feel the Superintendent's body vibrating with tension. "Why don't you do yourself a favour? You know it's all over. There's nowhere else to go. Don't make it worse for yourself."

"You make me laugh," the Boss sneered. "I'm holding all the aces, Mossy, so don't kid yourself."

Moss didn't seem even to have heard him. "Listen," he went on, "if you chuck it up now and come quietly, I'll put in a good word for you. I'll do what I can to talk your sentence down. But if you make me take you, by God you'll be sorry. What about it?"

"Go—yourself!" snarled the Boss, with a violent obscenity that made Gavin flinch.

Moss had been trying to inch forward as he spoke, but he saw James's finger shiver on the trigger, and realised he was too far gone to be reasoned with. He turned his attention instead to the younger man.

"What about you, son? Are you going to be sensible? Come on, Andy, we know all about you. You can't get away, you're going down one way or another, but you don't want to do longer than you have to, do you? Chuck it up now, and do yourself a favour. Don't let old Gentleman Jim talk you into a twenty-stretch. Let him do his own time."

Andy licked his lips uncertainly, and glanced at the Boss.

176

"He's right, Boss," he said. "We've had it. Let's chuck it up. We don't want anyone to get hurt—"

"*Shut up*! You snivelling little rat, shut your face!" the Boss yelled. "You try it and I'll shoot you first!"

"But Boss—"

In that instant, when the Boss's attention was distracted, Gavin caught Emma's eye. In the extraordinary tension of the moment, understanding flowed between them like a surge of electricity. Gavin felt the hair rise on his scalp. It was as if, just for that split second, each knew exactly what the other was thinking.

Andy's grip on Emma had slackened as his attention was focused on the Boss. It was enough for her. As she and Gavin exchanged that strange knowledge, she jabbed backwards with her elbows with all her strength, throwing her weight with them. Andy grunted with pain, and staggered, thrown off balance; Emma wrenched herself free, and made a break for it, running away from the group, sideways, away from the Boss.

Everything happened in a second. Andy staggered, the Boss thrust Poppy away from him as he took aim at Emma, and Gavin flung himself in one springing leap at the Boss's gun-arm.

Gavin's hands closed over the Boss's wrist. He felt the weight of the gun in the man's hand. He thrust the arm away from him, trying to push it upwards; and as the gun went off he felt the violent concussion a split second before he heard the explosion.

Gavin had been quick enough to spoil the Boss's aim, but not quick enough to prevent him firing. While the shot was still ringing on the quiet morning air, the rest of the police piled in, snatching Poppy away and overpowering both men. It was all over in the blinking of an eye; but to Gavin it seemed as though time had stopped, and he was frozen into immobility, staring at the crumpled figure of Emma, lying a few yards away, face down in the tussocky grass.

It was months before he managed to rid his memory of the image, and stop replaying in his dreams the moment when the shot rang out and she fell, and lay still, face down as she had fallen, in that terrible silence. He had known then that she was dead, that he had killed her, and his heart had died too in that moment.

He and another policeman reached her simultaneously. They could not have taken a second, for the pigeons were still rattling up from the trees, disturbed by the shot. Four eager hands turned her over; and then her eyes opened and she looked up at Gavin, and he felt sick with relief. "Emma," he said, and it was like a prayer, like thanksgiving.

"My leg," she whispered.

"She couldn't save herself," the policeman said, "because of her hands being tied." He was examining the wound. "I don't think it's too bad. Looks as if it's gone through the fleshy part. Bit of a mess," he added in a lower voice to Gavin, "but as long as the bone's not broken—"

"It hurts," Emma moaned.

"Don't worry, love, we'll get an ambulance to you right away," the policeman said, standing up; and to Gavin, "Stay with her, all right?"

Gavin didn't even hear him. He was busy working on the knot in the rope that tied her arms; then he remembered his knife, and got on quicker. He felt sick again at the sight of the ragged wounds on her wrists. "Oh Emma," he moaned, "what did they do to you?"

She looked up at him imploringly; he read her eyes and took her into his arms, holding her close against him. She shivered, feeling the terror of the past week begin to drain from her at last into the strength of his body. And then there were hurrying feet and a small, desperate voice crying, "*Gavin!*" and Poppy flung herself on them. Gavin opened up one arm and took her in too, and hugged them both tightly.

178

"I'll never let either of you out of my sight, ever again," he said. He held them tighter, and heard himself make a strange noise, like a sob, or a laugh of relief – perhaps both.

"Ambulance is on its way," came Superintendent Moss's voice from behind him. "And one of the lads is bringing up a first aid kit from one of the cars, see if we can dress that until it comes."

Gavin laid Emma back down on the grass, and looked up at the Superintendent. "Thank you for getting them back," he said, his whole heart in his voice.

"Couldn't have done it without you," Moss said kindly. "You've been a bloody nuisance, but you've been a great help too. And that was a brave thing you did, Miss Ruskin. Foolhardy, but brave."

"She's been brave all the time," Poppy said, garrulous with the relief and excitement of their rescue. "She's been so brave and clever you wouldn't believe! And those two men, I hope they go to prison for ever and ever! Poor Emma, does it hurt a lot? I'm so sorry to make all this trouble for you."

Emma tried to speak, to reassure her, but she was greying out with the pain. Gavin saw, and took hold of her hand, squeezing it hard. "Hold on to me," he said softly. "Not long now."

It seemed an eternity, the wait for the ambulance; but after a while Emma seemed to grow detached from it, so that she *knew* she was in pain rather than *felt* it. The rough grass under her, the open sky above her; the warmth of the sun on her face and the sound of birds and distant voices; all these drifted in and out of her consciousness as she floated a little out of her body. But Gavin's hand holding hers – the warmth and hardness of it, the shape of the palm and the impress of every finger – that was real. It was the point of contact which kept her tethered to the earth, and stopped her letting go and floating right away like a big, weightless, pain-filled balloon.

*   *   *

179

It wasn't until the afternoon that the hospital allowed the police in to take a preliminary statement; and even then, Emma was so drowsy with painkillers and shock that they did not stay long. Just a few points, they said, and they'd leave her to sleep. They could come back the next day for a more detailed statement.

Moss himself called in the next morning, to thank her again, and see how she was getting on.

"It hurts," she said briefly. She felt very low and rather tearful, which the nursing staff said was reaction to the fear and suspense of the past week. "What will happen to the Boss and Andy?"

"Twenty years, I should think," Moss said tersely. "Andy Luckmeed might get less, given that Harry James was the brains behind it; but neither of them will be seeing the light of day again for a long, long time."

It took hours to take her statement; she needed frequent breaks. The policemen went out obediently when the medical staff made their rounds, and again when the nurses came to take her temperature and give her painkillers. She bore it all stoically. She wanted them to have every detail that might put the two men away for a good, long time.

In the afternoon there was a very embarrassing visit from Mr Akroyd. He tiptoed in almost camouflaged with a vast bouquet of roses; and seeing she was awake, stood at the foot of the bed and looked at her, giving the impression that if he had been a cap-wearer, he would have been twisting it round and round in his hands.

"I want to thank you, Miss Ruskin," he said, "but I can't think of any words that would be enough. You saved my little girl. What can I say? Anything you want, anything at all, just name it – it's yours."

"You don't have to thank me," Emma said awkwardly.

"But I do," Mr Akroyd went on; and a surprising blush coloured his face. "And I have to apologise to you. When all this came out – well, the police said it must have been

180

an inside job, someone who knew the ropes, you see. And, not to beat about the bush, I thought it was you. You'd only been with us a few weeks. It seemed obvious that it must be you. Well, I was wrong, I admit it. I feel as bad as can be that it even crossed my mind. I hope you can forgive me."

"It's all right," Emma said. "It doesn't matter."

"It does matter." Mr Akroyd was not used to being contradicted. "It seems from what Superintendent Moss says that you've acted throughout the whole business with courage and resourcefulness, and that if it wasn't for you they'd never have found you both, or got you away from the kidnappers. It was all down to your guts and initiative that we got Poppy back. So whatever you want by way of a reward, it's all right with me. The sky's the limit – and I won't take no for an answer, so just think on! You can let me know what you've decided when you come home."

Emma was feeling very tired and the painkillers were wearing off again, and Mr Akroyd's belligerent determination to see himself in her debt made her feel tearful. She felt he wanted to pay her off, so that he needn't be under obligation to her, needn't think about her any more. And to call Long Hempdon 'home'! It was not her home, and never could be. She was glad when a nurse came in and chased him away.

That evening she had the visit she'd been waiting for. Gavin came in, weighted down with flowers, gifts, messages and cards.

"Hullo, how are you feeling?" he said. He put the whole armful down on the floor so that he could lean over and kiss her cheek. "You look tired. How's the leg?"

"Hurts like hell," she said. She was glad she didn't need to be polite about it, not to him.

He frowned and picked up her hand and kissed her bandaged wrist. "I don't know how we can ever repay you."

"Oh, don't you start," she said wearily. "I had your

father in earlier, threatening me with a reward, like a belligerent Father Christmas. I can't accept anything, you must know that."

Gavin smiled. "I'll talk to him, try and head him off. What did they say about your leg?"

"The doctor said the bullet passed right through the calf, which is the good news. If it had hit bone, I'd have been in a terrible mess. As it is, he says it will heal eventually, though I may be left with some permanent muscle damage."

Gavin looked stricken. "Oh Emma, what can I say? All this for our little girl!"

"How is she? How is Poppy?" Emma asked, knowing she'd get the truth from him. "I haven't seen her since the arrest."

"She's really wonderful. I can't believe how she's bounced back. She's so full of talk and self-confidence, you'd think she'd been on some kind of adventure holiday, rather than an ordeal like that. The only thing is—" he bit his lip. "She thinks you might blame her for what's happened to you."

"That's silly!"

"She thinks you won't come back. That's what's worrying Dad, as well. I know it must have been a dreadful experience for you, but I promised them both that I would ask you." He looked at her with a veiled, watchful expression. "When you're well, will you come back and teach her again?"

Emma looked at him, her heart a cold lump in her chest. In the woods he had held her close, and she had seen love and concern in his face; now he was wary, detached, non-committal. She was just an employee to him after all; she had been mistaken.

"No," she said, "I won't. I love Poppy dearly, as if she was my own sister – almost as if she was my daughter – but it isn't right. She needs to go to school and be with other children her own age, not to be shut up in that house all day with an adult. In the right school, she'll flourish – and I say this though it will make me very sad never to see her again, so you know how strongly I feel about it."

"Good," Gavin said, his face clearing. "I'm glad you feel like that, for two reasons. The first is that I have a plan for Poppy which I'm hoping to persuade my parents to agree to, and having your approval will make it easier. I want to enrol her in a school in London that I know of – the child of a friend of mine goes there, and he recommended it. I'm going to get a flat near by, so that she can be a day pupil and live with me during the week. And she can go home to Long Hempdon for weekends and holidays. What do you think?"

"I think it sounds pretty good." Emma was surprised. Mrs Grainger had said he was like a father to Poppy, but this seemed quite a sacrifice on his part. She wondered whether he would manage to look after a little girl all on his own. But of course, being rich he could afford a housekeeper, or whatever was needed. "How will that fit in with your work?" she asked.

"I've been offered a management job with a firm outside the group. It's based in London, and I'd like to take it for a couple of years, to get some experience before I step into the family business."

"Well, that seems to have worked out nicely, doesn't it," she said. And then, "You said there were two reasons. What's the second?"

Gavin looked at her almost timidly. He picked up her hand and stroked it. "You said that you'd be sorry never to see Poppy again. How would you like to really be her sister?" She stared at him. "I'm not making much of a job of this, am I?" he said with a rueful smile. "What I'm trying to say is that I love you, Emma. Will you marry me?"

"Marry you?" she whispered blankly.

"Oh my God, is it such a terrible prospect? Which of us is it you don't want to live with – me or Poppy? Tell me the truth – I can take it." He lifted her hand and put it to his cheek. "Look at me, clowning to cover up my nerves. Emma, put me out of my misery! Was I mistaken? I thought you cared for me."

"I do," she said suddenly, her poor overloaded brain catching up with her tongue at last. "I do – but – but do you really love me?"

"Madly. Entirely. Will you marry me?"

"Yes," she said.

"Yes?"

"Yes! Kiss me, you idiot!"

He didn't need asking twice. He kissed her long and thoroughly, and when he let her go, she only sighed and smiled at him. "I've waited so long for that," she murmured.

"Me too," he said. "D'you mind if I do it again?"

He came to visit her every day, and spent as much time with her as he could. Her leg was going to be a long time mending; it was lucky they had plenty to talk about. They told each other their side of events; Gavin told her, gravely, about Zara's involvement. She was shocked, but, on later reflection, not terribly surprised. Zara was being sent abroad for six months, to a Swiss academy to learn cordon bleu cookery. It was what Society people did with difficult girls, she learned.

She had other visitors too. Her parents came, in a state of delayed panic; Poppy and Mrs Henderson both came; Lady Susan almost did – she was moved enough to send a message of thanks and some grapes. The police came and reporters came – the hospital wasn't too pleased about that. And there were heaps of letters, cards and flowers, many of them from complete strangers.

"You're quite famous in a quiet sort of way," Gavin said.

"This is quiet?" she protested.

"You know what I mean. You're a heroine. Here, I promised to see you got this one." He distracted her with a large card, signed by her former flat-mates. "They were worried sick – saw the arrest in the papers. They want to know if they can come and visit you at the weekend."

"Of course! I'd love to see them. I do miss them. Have you spoken to them, then?"

"I called in yesterday when I was up in town."

"I suppose they were all over you? You made a big impression there, you know."

"They're nice. And I envied you so much, living like that."

"So tell me," Emma said, getting to a question she had long wanted to ask, "how come you were so affable and easy-going with them the first time you met them, and with me you were stiff and formal and practically hostile."

"I wasn't in love with them."

"Don't tease – I want to know."

"It's true – I fell in love with you almost the moment I met you."

"But you were so cold and aloof with me, I thought you despised me."

"It wasn't all my fault, you know. You were very brittle and uncompromising. You picked on me all the time. I thought you despised me."

She grinned. "So that's what you liked about me!"

"I'd never met anyone like you – you were so bull-headed and determined."

"How feminine you make me sound!"

"And when I found you loved Poppy, I loved you even more. And then you disappeared and I thought, if I should lose you—" He stopped. "I don't ever want to go through anything like that again."

They were silent, and he saw that he had made her relive it, and was sorry. To lighten the mood he said, "Would you mind living in the house in Mayfair for a short time after we're married? Just until we get a flat?"

"No, I suppose not. Why?"

185

He grinned. "I promised the girls we'd have them to dinner there."

"You like them that much?" she laughed.

"I like them so much, I think they ought to be your bridesmaids, along with Poppy, of course – and Zara if you can stand her."

"Five bridesmaids trooping along behind a limping bride? It'd have the congregation in stitches," Emma said. "Are you sure we have to have a big wedding?"

"I'm afraid so. My stepmother and all her friends will expect it. Penalty of being rich: you can't just please yourself."

"Oh well, I suppose I can survive it," she said, and looked up at him with a smile which said she could survive anything as long as he was there with her. Then she laughed. "I've just thought of something."

"What?"

"If I marry a millionaire's son and heir—"

"Yes?"

"How will Suzanne ever be able to forgive me?"